TORRENT

ANTHONY B. GRAY

For C and J who make everything worthwhile.

Love,

Dad

PREFACE

Life's deepest wounds often birth our most powerful stories. As an attorney, I'm trained to seek order in chaos, to find logic in human conflict. But when my own marriage crumbled, no legal precedent could guide me through the darkness of loss and self-reflection. This story emerged from those shadows – a thriller that explores how grief can blind us, how love can both destroy and redeem us, and how sometimes we must lose everything to find ourselves. Through Samuel's journey in Canyon Park, I confronted my own demons, discovering that healing rarely follows a linear path.

PROLOGUE

The river flows eternal through Canyon Park, carving stories into stone. Some say these waters hold secrets - of love lost, of dreams drowned, of souls seeking redemption among the towering cliffs. But darkness lurks in these depths, wearing many faces. For decades, women have vanished along these trails, their disappearances dismissed as tragic accidents. Search parties comb the wilderness, and eventually, the mountains keep their silence. The river continues its endless journey, washing away evidence like tears. Two women will enter these canyons, unaware they're being hunted. A grieving widower will follow, carrying his own ghosts into the wilderness. And predators will welcome them all, as they have so many others, with practiced smiles and deadly intent. But this time, the river has different plans. This time, the mountains will not keep their silence.

CONTENTS

CHAPTER 1

WHEN MONICA LEFT

"I can't believe she's not answering her phone!" Samuel slammed his hand against the steering wheel of his Mercedes S-Class as he pulled into the driveway of their three-story townhome. The modern glass and steel structure stood proudly in Atlanta's trendy Beltway district – a testament to his meteoric rise at Gates and Tate, PLLC, one of the Southeast's premier law firms.

Monica had wanted a ranch house in the suburbs, somewhere in Cobb or DeKalb County. "A place where children can grow," she'd said. But after the miscarriage, Samuel had shut down that conversation. He wanted to travel, to enjoy the fruits of his labor. Another round of IVF treatments or the astronomical costs of surrogacy were not part of his carefully plotted five-year plan.

As the garage door hummed open, he spotted Mrs. Hines hovering over her perpetually dying rose bushes. The retired schoolteacher was already power walking toward his driveway, pruning shears in hand like a botanical weapon.

"Oh God," Samuel muttered. Monica always indulged the woman, bonding over their shared teaching backgrounds and discussing everything from fertilizer to foreign policy. But Samuel saw her for what she was – a lonely widow desperate for connection, even if it meant prying into others' lives.

"Samuel! Samuel!" Mrs. Hines called out, her voice carrying that tone of elderly concern that set his teeth on edge. "I've been trying to reach Monica all day!"

"Join the club," he mumbled, willing the garage door to close faster.

Mrs. Hines wedged herself into the narrowing gap. "She hasn't answered her door either. I'm worried about the pitiful thing. She's been so down lately since the..." she trailed off, eyes dropping to the concrete, "well, you know."

"Thank you, Mrs. Hines." Samuel's practiced courtroom smile felt brittle. "I'm sure everything's fine. Have a nice day now." He jabbed the door button repeatedly, watching with satisfaction as she backed away from the descending barrier.

Inside his car, Samuel exhaled deeply. He gathered his case files from the passenger seat, where they mingled with empty protein shake bottles and crumpled energy bar wrappers. Monica hated his mobile office approach, but he needed everything within reach. Time was billable, after all.

The door connecting the garage to the house opened into their meticulously decorated foyer. Samuel dropped his sport coat and briefcase on the ottoman, ignoring Monica's rule about keeping the entry clear.

"Monica?" His voice echoed through the empty space. "Monica, where are you?"

The sound of running water drifted down from upstairs. Another one of her endless "self-care" baths, no doubt. Samuel rolled his eyes

at the concept. Self-care was just therapist-speak for avoiding responsibility. He managed his own stress simply fine – early morning HIT
, twelve-hour workdays, networking events. He pushed through, like
adults were supposed to.

But something felt wrong. The water had been running too long,
and there was a strange quality to the silence beneath it. As he looked
up, Samuel noticed a discolored patch on the ceiling, water seeping
through the pristine white paint.

"What the hell? Monica!"

He took the stairs two at a time, expensive loafers squeaking on
the hardwood. The hallway to their primary suite seemed to stretch
endlessly, and when he reached the bedroom, his feet squelched into
the soaked carpet.

Water was streaming under the barn door that separated the bedroom from the primary bath. Samuel's irritation evaporated, replaced
by a creeping dread that turned his bones to ice.

"Monica?" His voice came out barely above a whisper. He removed
his shoes, each movement suddenly needing immense effort, as if he
were trying to walk through molasses.

She had threatened this before. He had dismissed it as atten-
tion-seeking, as weakness. But now, facing that closed door with water
pooling around his feet, those moments replayed in his mind with
horrifying clarity.

His hand slipped on the door handle; palms slick with sweat. The
door felt impossibly heavy as he pushed it open, water rushing past his
feet like a miniature tide.

A thousand thoughts crashed through his mind. This morning
had been off – no coffee made, no gentle humming as she watered
her plants before she headed to her kindergarten class. He had been
too preoccupied with his upcoming deposition to really look at her,

just dropped a perfunctory kiss on her cheek before rushing out. Last night's argument about surrogacy costs rang in his ears. He'd been so certain about his position, so dismissive of her desires.

His heart thundered in his ears like a tribal drum as the door swung wide. Dark hair floated in the overflowing tub like seaweed, and Samuel felt his throat close completely. He moved forward on autopilot, reaching to turn off the faucet with numb fingers.

"No," he breathed. "No, no, no. You wouldn't do this. You couldn't."

He fell to his knees beside the tub, hands shaking as he lifted her face from the water. Her eyes were vacant, rolled back, lips blue against skin that had once glowed with life. Angry red lines scored on her wrists, the water around them stained rust brown.

"Oh babe," he choked out, "why? Why?"

But he knew why. He had always known why. He just had not wanted to listen.

Samuel stumbled backward from the tub; his designer suit soaked where he'd touched her. His legs gave out and he slid down the bathroom wall, fumbling for his phone with numb fingers. Water dripped from his sleeves, each drop echoing like a gavel strike in the now-silent bathroom.

"911, what's your emergency?" "My wife..." His lawyer's voice, the one that commanded courtrooms, cracked like a teenager's. "She's... the bathtub... I can't..."

"Sir, is your wife breathing?"

The question hit him like a physical blow. Monica. Breathing. His Monica. The same Monica who hummed while watering her plants every morning. Who smiled even through tears after the miscarriage. Who he'd barely looked at over breakfast.

"No," he whispered. "She's not... I can't... oh God, Monica..."

"Sir, I'm dispatching emergency services. Stay on the line with me. Did you try to—"

"She's gone!" The words tore from his throat. "She's gone, and I didn't... I never... I was too busy with the Jensen merger to see..." His voice dissolved into sounds he'd never heard himself make before. Water continued trickling onto the marble floor, spreading like guilt around his Italian leather shoes.

The 911 operator's voice faded to a distant hum as his eyes fixed on Monica's hand hanging over the tub's edge, her wedding ring catching the light. When was the last time he'd really held that hand? Sirens wailed in the distance as Samuel forced himself up. What did one do when their world drowned? His feet carried him to their bedroom on autopilot, leaving wet footprints on the plush carpet Monica had chosen. The bed was perfectly made, hospital corners crisp – one final act of order in her disordered world.

***

A single sheet of paper lay centered on her pillow, her handwriting immediately striking him as foreign.

"My dearest Samuel, I've been slipping away for so long, and you, my love, haven't even noticed. Every morning, I wake up and try to keep going, but I'm so tired of trying alone. The miscarriage broke something in me, yes. But your refusal to try again, to even consider another round of IVF – that showed me how differently we see our future. You calculate odds and weigh options while I crumble. You schedule mergers while I disappear in silence. I love you. I've loved you since that first coffee date when you spoke about justice with such passion. I still love you, even

now. But I can't keep living in a world where numbers matter more than dreams, where case files are more urgent than my breaking heart. Remember how I used to beg you to go camping? To step away from your carefully controlled world? Maybe if you had, you would have seen me fading. Maybe you would have noticed that your bright, laughing Monica was already gone. I don't blame you, my logical love. We're simply different creatures – you thrive in the ordered world of law, while I needed the realm of emotion and connection. I just wish, one time, you had put down your case files long enough to truly see me. Take care of my plants. They need attention to thrive, just like people do.

   All my love, Monica"

***

The paper crumpled in Samuel's shaking hands as emergency vehicles screamed to a stop outside. Red and blue lights strobed through the windows, painting the bedroom in colors of crisis.

"Sir?" The 911 operator's voice still emanated from his fallen phone. "Emergency services are arriving. Can you open the door?" Samuel's legs buckled. He hit the carpet hard, Monica's last words clutched to his chest. Memories crashed over him like waves: her untouched dinner plates as she picked at her food. The growing silence in their home. Her tearful plea last week about trying one more IVF cycle.

He'd dismissed it as emotional manipulation, too focused on billable hours to see she was going under. The front door burst open downstairs. Boots thundered up the stairs as Samuel knelt there, drowning in his own delayed grief. His analytical mind tried desperately to categorize this moment, to file it away like case law, but there was no precedent for this level of guilt. No motion he could file to turn back time.

"Up here!" he tried to call out, but what emerged was more primal – a howl of recognition that he hadn't just failed to save his drowning wife. He had been the weight that pulled her under. Heavy footsteps approached the bedroom as Samuel rocked back and forth, still clutching Monica's note. His last shred of professional composure dissolved as paramedics and police swarmed past him toward the bathroom.

In their wake, water from his soaked clothes seeped into the carpet, spreading like the realization that his carefully ordered world had just drowned alongside his wife.

CHAPTER 2

Deaths Paperwork

The coroner's van sat in the driveway like a white herald of death, its bold lettering seeming to mock Samuel with its institutional cheerfulness. Inside his home, people in masks and blue booties moved with practiced efficiency, like worker ants serving some unseen queen. Their whispered conversations and rubber-soled footsteps created a surreal symphony of loss.

The late fall sun was setting behind the Tudor-style houses across the street, its dying rays catching the weeping willow's branches and transforming them into strings of nature's Christmas lights. A crowd had gathered on the sidewalk, their murmured conversations carrying across the manicured lawn. Mrs. Hines stood at the bottom of the front steps, gathering courage to approach, but Samuel kept his eyes fixed on the hardwood floor. Eye contact would be an invitation he could not bear to extend.

"Sir, Mr. Ross, I think we're almost done here."

Samuel looked up to find a petite blonde officer standing before him. Her kind eyes held that particular blend of professional detachment and personal sympathy reserved for the newly bereaved.

"Mr. Ross, we'll need you to make an official statement to close out our case." The officer's gaze slid away from his face, unable to keep contact with his raw grief.

"It's Samuel, please call me Samuel." His voice caught. "What will you do with her... with her body?" A tear escaped before he could stop it, its salt burning a path down his cheek. "I'm sorry!"

"Sir, please don't apologize. You've been through a trauma, and any response is appropriate." The officer pulled a white business card from her folder, placing it on the round coffee table with deliberate care. "When you're ready, give me a call to make your statement. I also have a number for a grief counselor—"

"Counseling?" Samuel shot up from his chair, his six-foot frame towering over the officer. "Like the counseling Monica was getting?" Anger surged through him, hot and sudden. "Some fucking help that did, right?" He caught himself rising onto his tiptoes, ready to launch into full courtroom mode, then deflated just as quickly. "Sorry... I didn't mean..."

"Sir, no problem—"

"Samuel. Please." The word came out sharper than intended.

"Yes, Samuel." The officer's eyes drifted to the bay window, where their wedding photo sat in its silver frame. Monica's face beamed with vitality; her pearl-white mermaid dress perfectly fitted as she leaned into his arm. Even his younger self's characteristic smirk seemed a betrayal now, a reminder of how blind he had been to her pain.

"Have you contacted anyone? Family? Friends?"

Samuel sank deeper into his chair. "Not yet. I haven't called her mother. Her brother's coming down from DC tomorrow. I still need to call Collette, her best friend, and her school..." His voice trailed off as he realized each call would force him to relive this moment, to explain the unexplainable.

"Samuel, one more thing, the note you found on the bed. We'll need to take it for our files, but we'll return it once we've made a copy. Would you happen to have any other examples of her handwriting for comparison?" The officer asked delicately.

"Her grade book. She teaches – taught – kindergarten at Rosa Parks Academy." He jumped up, glad for any excuse to move. "I can get it—"

"That can wait until you come in for your statement." The officer was already planning her exit, and Samuel wondered if this was just another routine call for her. She was a rookie, cutting her teeth on suicides the way young journalists started with obituaries.

"I don't want the note," he said abruptly. He had no intention of reading it again, ever. The miscarriage had broken something in their marriage, in Monica, and he was not ready to face her ultimate thoughts on the matter.

The officer moved toward the door, casting one last professional glance up the stairs. A nod from the coroner's assistant signaled it was time. "Samuel, they're ready to bring her down. Would you prefer they use the back door, for privacy?"

Privacy? Samuel almost laughed. What privacy could there be with that branded van sitting in the driveway like a circus tent? His muscles tensed as anger surged again – anger at Monica for putting him in this position, for making him decide whether her body should be paraded past the neighbors or smuggled out like contraband.

The back porch was barely large enough for a lawn chair and his cold plunge tank. They would still have to circle around to the front, past all the gawking faces.

"Um... I don't know. What do you think?" He stared through the front door's glass panel at the growing crowd of spectators.

"That's not my decision," the officer said gently, rising on tiptoes to pat his shoulder. "Why don't we use the garage?"

Samuel retreated to his home office, bracing himself against his desk. His law degree hung centered on the wall, its gold lettering catching the last rays of sunlight. He gripped the desk's edge as if preparing for a physical blow. "Okay. Do it now."

Time stretched like taffy as the coroner's assistants descended the stairs, their footsteps marking each step with terrible precision. The off-white bag reminded him perversely of Monica's wedding dress, but where that day had been filled with joy and anticipation, this procession carried only sorrow and averted gazes.

Samuel stared at his credentials on the wall, unable to watch. At their wedding, all eyes had been drawn to Monica's radiance. Now, everyone seemed desperate to look anywhere else as they carried her lifeless body through his pristine kitchen and into the garage.

"We're done here," the officer said softly. "Take your time. Come to the station when you're ready."

And then they were gone, leaving Samuel alone with the deafening silence of his empty house and the weight of all his unspoken regrets.

CHAPTER 3

Memories In Boxes

"You don't have to pack up everything now," Collette said as she stood in Monica's and Samuel's primary bedroom closet, watching him methodically strip hangers with mechanical precision.

"The sooner it's done, the better," Samuel replied curtly, not breaking his rhythm.

Each garment was efficiently folded, placed in boxes labeled 'Donate' with his precise legal handwriting. Collette opened the closet's built-in drawers, handling each item like a fragile artifact. Her hands froze on a leather-bound book hidden beneath Monica's sweaters.

"Oh God," she whispered.

"What?" Samuel glanced over, irritation plain on his face.

"Her baby book." Collette's voice cracked. "The one she started when..." She opened it carefully, revealing Monica's flowing handwriting. Nursery color schemes. Name lists. An ultrasound photo labeled "Our Miracle" with a heart.

"Just put it in the trash pile," Samuel muttered, turning back to his hangers.

"Trash pile?" Collette's voice sharpened. "She was six months pregnant, Samuel. She spent three months in bed after losing the baby, while you... you just kept going to work like nothing happened."

"What was I supposed to do? Stop billing hours? Let my cases collapse?" Samuel's professional mask slipped, revealing raw anger underneath. "She made her choice. She gave up."

"Gave up?" Collette clutched the book to her chest. "I sat with her every day while you were at the office. She wasn't giving up – she was drowning in grief, and you couldn't be bothered to notice."

"Don't." Samuel's voice turned cold. "You don't get to judge how I handled my wife's death."

"Your wife's death?" Collette's laugh held no humor. "What about her life, Samuel? When was the last time you saw her? Really saw her?" She flipped pages in the book.

"Look – she had the nursery planned down to the lamp shades. While you were working on whatever important lawyer stuff you were doing, she was picking out tiny clothes and writing letters to a baby she'd never meet."

Samuel's hands stilled on a silk blouse.

"She knew how important my work was—"

"More important than her? Than your child?" Collette's voice rose. "God, you're still doing it. Still justifying putting everything else first."

"I was providing for our future!" Samuel spun to face her. "Making partner meant security, meant we could try IVF again when the timing was right—"

"The timing?" Collette stepped closer, brandishing the book. "She lost her baby, Samuel. Your baby. There is no right timing for that kind of pain. But instead of grieving with her, you hid in your office. Instead of holding her, you held case files."

"You think I don't know that?" Samuel's voice cracked. "You think I don't replay every moment, wondering if I could have..." He caught himself, the professional mask sliding back into place.

"It doesn't matter now. She made her decision."

"No, Samuel. You made yours long before she made hers." Collette placed the baby book deliberately on the bed.

"You decided your career mattered more than her heart. You decided billable hours were more important than her pain."

Samuel's jaw clenched as he turned back to the closet. "Are you done psychoanalyzing me? I have a lot to get through here."

"That's exactly what I mean." Collette shook her head. "Even now, you're treating this like another task to complete. Efficient. Organized. Everything in its proper box." She picked up a framed photo of Monica by the lake.

"She used to beg you to go camping, you know. To step away from your precious routine and just be present with her."

"Monica knew who I was when she married me," Samuel said tightly.

"Did she? Or did she know who you could have been?" Collette's voice softened. "The man who talked about justice with such passion in college. The one who used to say laws existed to protect people, not profits?"

"Enough." Samuel braced his hands against the closet doorframe. "What do you want from me, Collette? Monica's gone. No amount of dredging up the past will change that."

"No, but it might change you." Collette moved to the bedroom window, looking out at Monica's neglected garden. "That's why I'm here, actually. Not just to help pack up her life into neat little boxes."

Samuel's shoulders tensed. "What does that mean?"

"I booked a trip," Collette turned to face him. "To Canyon Park. Monica and I were supposed to go in April." She watched his reaction carefully.

"She loved that place. Used to go there with her father." "I know about Canyon Park," Samuel said dismissively. "She mentioned it. Several times."

"Mentioned it?" Collette's voice took on an edge again. "She begged you to go there with her. To share something, she loved. But you were always too busy, weren't you? Another motion to file, another brief to prepare."

Samuel began sorting clothes again with sharp, angry movements. "What's your point?"

"I think you should come. Instead of Monica." The words hung in the air between them. Samuel's laugh was harsh. "A camping trip? Now? I have work—"

"Of course you do." Collette picked up the baby book again. "You always have work. You had work when she was pregnant. Work when she lost the baby. Work when she needed you most."

She opened a page where Monica had written "Our Family Adventures" with small drawings of hiking trails and campfires. "Work right up until she decided she couldn't compete with your legal work anymore." The silence stretched between them, heavy with accusation and grief. Samuel's hands stilled on Monica's favorite sweater – the soft blue one she'd worn their last morning together.

"She would have wanted you to go," Collette said quietly. "To finally see what she tried to show you all those years. To understand why she loved it there."

Samuel's analytical mind raced through objections: court schedules, client meetings, the Thompson deposition. But underneath, in a place he usually kept carefully walled off, another voice whispered.

Monica's voice, from their last breakfast: "I can't keep hoping while you calculate odds..."

"I'll think about it," he found himself saying, surprising them both. Collette nodded, placing the baby book carefully in the 'Keep' box.

"That's more consideration than you usually gave her plans." She headed for the door, then paused. "You know, Samuel, for a man who built his career on fighting for justice, you never seemed to notice the injustice happening right in your own home."

The words hit him like a physical blow. He waited until her footsteps faded down the stairs before sinking onto the bed – Monica's side, still made with hospital corners even on her last morning. The Thompson deposition could be rescheduled. The Martinez brief could wait. Maybe... it was time to step away from his carefully controlled world. Even if just for a few days.

Samuel stared at the 'Keep' box containing the baby book, his mind wandering to the last real conversation he'd had with Monica. Not the brief morning exchanges about coffee and schedules, but an actual conversation. He couldn't remember one. His perfectly ordered mind, capable of recalling case law from decades ago, couldn't produce a single meaningful dialogue with his wife from the past months.

The sound of Collette rummaging through the kitchen downstairs drifted up – sorting through Monica's cookbook collection. Those elaborate meals she'd planned, trying to entice him home earlier. How many had grown cold on the dinner table while he worked late? He pulled out his phone, muscle memory taking him to his calendar. The neat blocks of time, perfectly allocated to depositions, client meetings, court appearances – his ordered world in digital form. Monica had lived somewhere in the margins of those blocks, in the spaces between appointments.

"Dammit," he muttered, dropping the phone on the bed. Collette's words echoed: "for a man who built his career on fighting for justice..." His fingers found Monica's sweater again, the soft blue fabric still holding a trace of her lavender lotion. A camping trip. The very idea was absurd. He was a lawyer, not some outdoorsman. His idea of roughing it was a hotel without room service. But Monica loved it. Canyon Park especially. He remembered her face lighting up when she talked about the trails, the river, the stars at night. He'd always nodded abstractly, already thinking about his next case.

"Samuel?" Collette's voice carried up the stairs. Collette softened, guilt tempering her harsh judgment. "Monica loved hiking," Collette said softly.

"Yeah, she was crazy about the outdoors," Samuel replied mechanically. "I didn't share her love of nature, but I appreciated the physical challenge." He paused, staring out the window as if seeing something beyond the manicured suburban landscape.

"The trip is four days, right?" Samuel said, still looking out the window.

"Yeah, four days, three nights. Perfect early spring weather. Might even get to swim in the Canyon River." Collette flashed her practiced smile, deploying the charm she had always used to bend men to her will.

"The river would be nice," he managed a weak laugh. "But I've got so much work to catch up on, and..." His voice caught, emotion finally cracking through his carefully maintained facade.

"Hey, I'm sorry. I shouldn't have mentioned it." Collette touched his arm as she walked back up to the bedroom, surprising herself with the gesture. "Samuel, you know this isn't your fault."

But even as she said it, she knew she didn't fully believe it. Samuel forced a smile, guilt radiating from him in almost visible waves. Outside, clouds swept across the sun, casting the bedroom in shadows – nature itself seeming to mirror the darkness between them.

"Yup...ok I'll go," he said flatly, and walked out, leaving Collette alone with Monica's memories and questions she was not ready to answer.

He had no way of knowing that this decision – this small crack in his professional armor – would lead him into a nightmare where legal expertise meant nothing, and justice required more than carefully worded arguments.

CHAPTER 4

Woman In Purple

Samuel wedged his 6'ft muscular frame into the cramped window seat, muttering under his breath. A three-hour flight to California stretched before him like an eternity. He silently prayed for a small, quiet seat-mate – anything to avoid the inevitable battle for the middle armrest.

His hopes evaporated as a tall, fit man with carefully styled brown hair strode purposefully toward row sixteen. Something about him seemed familiar, like a face from the gym half-remembered.

"Hey man, I think we're sitting together!" The man bounded into the seat with puppy-like enthusiasm. Samuel suddenly placed him – Daniel, Shannon's boyfriend, from the HIT gym. Another reminder of the life he was trying to leave behind.

Daniel wore a tight Under Armor hoodie and athletic pants with white stripes – clothes clearly chosen to suggest more muscle than they held. Samuel found himself automatically comparing their builds, noting with grim satisfaction that his own physique was significantly more defined.

"It's me, Daniel – Shannon's boyfriend? From Uptown HIT?"

"Yeah, Daniel, I remember." Samuel's voice was flat. "Excited about the trip?"

"Oh man, so pumped to get into those mountains! Get away from the Atlanta grind, you know what I mean? "Daniel said.

Samuel turned toward the window, already regretting his decision to come. He had always looked down on Daniel – the perpetual bartender/construction worker who never seemed to settle into a real career. Just another of Monica's friend Shannon's rotating cast of boyfriends.

"Hey," Daniel's voice softened, "I never got to say how sorry I am about Monica. She was amazing. Shannon always said—"

"Yeah, well, these things happen," Samuel cut him off sharply. "It's been six months. Nothing to do but move forward." He caught himself, surprised by his own vulnerability. What was it about Daniel's earnest demeanor that made him want to lower his guard? He quickly redirected his attention to the air vent, rebuilding his walls.

"Canyon Park is supposed to be beautiful," Daniel pressed on. "Shannon went with Monica and Collette a couple years back. The trails look incredible in the videos—"

"Yeah, should be fun." Samuel's tone made it clear the conversation was over.

"Shannon and Collette are sitting together," Daniel chuckled nervously. "Crazy, right? Shannon said she wanted to sit with Collette, but I think she just didn't want to sit with me."

Samuel bit back his agreement. "You know how women are. Look, I'm probably going to try to sleep."

"Oh yeah, totally. Enjoy the last air conditioning we'll see for a while, right?" Daniel's laugh faded as he noticed Samuel had already closed his eyes, headphones firmly in place.

The dream came quickly:

Samuel walked along Canyon River's shore, the water an impossible shade of blue-green, currents racing beneath its surface like living things. The sun hung perfectly round in a cloudless sky, casting the canyon walls in shades of amber and rust. The mountains rose behind him, ancient and indifferent to human concerns.

The water flowed with urgent purpose, as if late for some cosmic appointment. As Samuel followed its path, a figure appeared on the opposite bank – a woman in a flowing purple dress that caught the breeze like a sail. Her dark hair barely brushed her shoulders, and she moved with an otherworldly grace, as if dancing to music only she could hear.

Samuel raised his hand, calling out, but his voice seemed to dissolve in the air between them. She continued her ethereal dance, perfectly mirroring his path along the shore but never acknowledging his presence. Her face remained turned away, hidden like a secret he wasn't meant to know.

Desperate to reach her, Samuel stepped into the water. The bottom dropped away immediately; the river far deeper than its clarity suggested. He kept sinking, expecting to find purchase on rocks or sand, but there was only the endless descent into blue-green infinity—

"Dude, you're snoring pretty hard there."

Samuel jerked awake, his throat raw and mouth dry. Daniel's concerned face swam into focus.

"Man, you were sawing some serious lumber. Thought you might mess with the cabin pressure," Daniel tried a joke.

"Haven't been sleeping well lately," Samuel muttered, already trying to recapture the dream, to see the woman's face. But like water through his fingers, it slipped away.

"Oh man, of course – with everything you've been through—"

"It's fine." Samuel checked his watch. Two hours remained. He closed his eyes again, but the dream was gone, replaced by the drone of engines and Daniel's nervous energy beside him.

The woman in purple lingered at the edges of his consciousness, just out of reach – like Monica herself had been in those final weeks, when he had been too blind to see her slipping away. Samuel pressed his forehead against the cool window, wondering if this trip was pulling him toward something or letting him run away.

Either way, the mountains were waiting, and somewhere in their shadows were answers he was not sure he wanted to find.

CHAPTER 5

DANGEROUS ATTRACTIONS

The fluorescent lights of Sacramento International Airport cast everyone in a sickly pallor, but somehow Collette still managed to glow. Samuel watched her work her magic on two men by the baggage claim, her practiced laugh carrying across the terminal. She wielded her beauty like a skilled fencer's blade, precise and purposeful. Samuel knew this dance well – Collette never flirted without an agenda.

Meanwhile, Shannon nestled into Daniel's side, their casual intimacy a stark reminder of what Samuel had lost. She was younger than Collette and Monica, with a nurse's compassion that sometimes hit too close to home. There was something of Monica in her – not physically, but in the way she carried her heart so openly. When she caught Samuel watching and offered a warm wave, he quickly turned away, busying himself with the endless parade of luggage on the carousel.

"Finally!" He spotted his blue bag, marked with white string – a practical system Monica had insisted upon. The memory stung as he hefted the bag off the belt, wondering what exactly he had gotten himself into. The weight of his decision to come felt heavier than any piece of luggage.

Collette sauntered over, trailing her new conquests like faithful puppies. "Hey, this is Mike and Andrew. They know a great bar near Canyon Park."

Her smile held that gleam that meant she'd already sized them up and found a use for them. Shannon perked up, ever the optimist. "Oh, that sounds cool! Do they have decent food?"

"You bet, the best BBQ around," the one called Mike answered with his arms folded across his chest. "Actually, you're not the first sorority group we've seen heading to Canyon Park. Seems to be a popular spot lately."

Samuel's jaw tightened. "Seriously?" The word came out sharper than intended, heavy with his growing irritation at this whole situation. He grabbed his camping backpack, eager to put distance between himself and this transparent attempt at a hookup.

"Well, we aren't girls," Collette corrected, her voice taking on that edge she used to prove dominance. "We're grown women. The hiking tour company markets to sororities – that's how we found them." She threaded her arm through Mike's – or was it, Andrew's? – making her choice clear.

Samuel walked away without looking back, his footsteps echoing against the terminal's polished floors. Already the pull of home – of his ordered, predictable life – tugged at him. But home meant an empty house, a pristine bathtub he couldn't bring himself to clean, and a closet half-full of clothes he couldn't bring himself to pack away.

At least in these mountains, his ghosts might have some competition.

Behind him, Collette's laughter rang out again, somehow both genuine and calculated. She'd always been good at playing both sides

– the carefree spirit and the careful strategist. It was what had drawn him to her in college before Monica. Before everything.

Shannon called after him, "Samuel, wait up!" But he kept walking, pretending not to hear. Her kindness was too reminiscent of Monica's, and right now, kindness feels more dangerous than any mountain trail.

The airport's automatic doors slid open, and the California heat hit him like a physical wall. Somewhere out there, Canyon Park waited with its secrets and challenges. Whatever Collette's motives were for bringing him here, whatever demons he was running from or toward, it was too late to turn back now.

The woman from his dream flickered at the edges of his memory – her purple dress, her dancing grace, her hidden face. He adjusted his pack and stepped into the heat, leaving the sound of Collette's orchestrated flirtation behind.

The mountains rose in the distance, their shadows already reaching for him like grasping fingers. Or like welcoming arms. He wasn't sure which would be worse.

CHAPTER 6

PREDATOR'S DANCE

The alarm blared as Buck reached over and tried to swat at it to stop. Buck's chiseled frame sprawled across the bed, his 6'4 body barely contained by the tangled sheets. Sunlight glinted off his tousled blond hair as he groaned, fighting the pounding headache from last night's excess. His muscular 245-pound physique rippled as he stretched, admiring his bulging biceps with a self-satisfied smirk. Despite the hangover, Buck could not help but appreciate his own Adonis-like reflection in the mirror. He knew he was God's gift to women-and the world. With a dramatic sigh, he contemplated gracing humanity with this presence. After all, they should consider themselves lucky to even catch a glimpse of his perfection.

"Shit! Tim...Tim!" Buck yelled outside of his room as he stood in the middle of the bedroom floor in his boxer shorts. "Tim where the fuck are you! Why didn't you wake me up?" "What good are you, Buck said to himself as he caught a glimpse of himself in the mirror on the dresser. He stopped and examined his biceps and chest and gave a quick flex.

Buck stormed into the kitchen, his massive frame dwarfing Tim, who stood by the coffee maker. "You little runt!" Buck snarled, looming over his brother. "Why didn't you wake me up?"

Tim stuttered, "I-I tried, Buck, but you- "

"Shut it, pipsqueak," Buck interrupted, snatching the coffee pot. "Bet you couldn't even budge me, huh? Pathetic." He sneered, flexing his bicep. "See this? This is what a real man looks like. Not some twig like you."

Tim's shoulders slumped as Buck continued, "Maybe if you weren't such a scrawny loser, you could've done something useful for once. Now move, before I use you as a toothpick."

Buck walked back to his room and went and grabbed his laptop. Buck's fingers drummed across his laptop keyboard, the blue glow illuminating his chiseled features. His eyes widened, and a wolfish grin spread across his face. "Well, well, well" he muttered, leaning back in his chair, "This is going to be a good one. Real-good. "He slammed the laptop shut with a sharp laugh that held no warmth.

"Timmy Boy!" Buck's deep voice boomed through the apartment. "Get your scrawny ass ready! We're going out!" He strode to Tim's doorway, filling the entire frame with his massive shoulders. Finding Tim reading a book, Buck snorted. "Jesus Christ, you're such a nerd. Tell me, how do you manage to look even more pathetic every time I see you?"

Tim looked up hopefully at the invitation to go out. "Really? You want me to come along?"

"Yeah, might as well bring my comic relief," Buck sneered. "But for God's sake, take a shower first. Maybe put on something that makes you look like a man, you puss." He chuckled at Tim's hurt expression. "Though that might take a miracle."

CHAPTER 7

BEAUTIFUL WEBS

Samuel nursed his scotch, watching Collette hold court at their table like some self-appointed queen of grief. Her perfectly manicured hands kept touching her sorority necklace she wore to honor her sorority sister Monica. Everything about this "healing journey" was just another excuse for Collette to make herself the center of attention.

The bar reeked of stale beer and broken dreams, filled with locals who thought Canyon River was the center of the universe. Just like Monica thought a baby would fix everything. Now here he sat, wrapped in this ridiculous facade of remembrance, when he should be preparing for next week's merger case.

Shannon and Daniel, the picture-perfect couple Collette had dragged along, couldn't keep their hands off each other. Their nauseating display of affection made his stomach turn. They kept whispering and giggling like teenagers, planning their perfect little future. Samuel wanted to tell them how it really ends-with one person leaving the other holding nothing but guilt and a stack of medical bills.

Samuel, you've barely touched your food." Collette chided, reaching across the table touching his hand. He pulled back, watching her practiced pout appear. Even in mourning, she couldn't help but flirt. Monica had always defended her attention seeking behavior, calling it "free-spirited." Look where that friendship had gotten them.

"I'm not hungry," he replied flatly, checking his phone again. "Some of us have actual responsibilities to return to."

The group fell silent, exactly what he wanted. Now they'd stop pretending this forced camping trip would somehow make everything okay.

A heavy wooden door swung open, and Buck strode in like he was walking onto a stage. His tight blue t-shirt strained against his chest, and his fitted ripped jeans showed off his athletic build. Behind him, Tim shuffled in, practically disappearing in his oversized plaid shirt, his messy man bun making him look more like a lost art student than a hiking guide.

"Well, hello beautiful." Buck's deep voice carried across the bar as he leaned onto the counter, flashing a practiced smile at the bartender, Jenny. She barely glanced up, having dealt with his routine countless times before. Tim hovered awkwardly behind his brother, perpetually in his shadow.

"What'll it be, Buck?" Jenny asked flatly, already reaching for a glass.

Buck's eyes scanned the room like a predator sizing up prey. "First, sweetheart, why don't you tell me who's new in town? Got any fresh faces I should know about?" He winked, running a hand through his perfectly styled blond hair.

Jenny stopped mid-pour, fixing him with a hard stare. "Really? We're doing this again. You know I don't play your creepy little games."

"Aw, come on, Jenny," Buck persisted, his charm never wavering. "I'm just trying to be a good host. Got a group coming through tomorrow for a trek, thought I might spot some of my clients."

"Buck—-"Tim started to interject, but Buck silenced him with a sharp look.

Jenny slammed the glass down. "Listen here, you oversized Ken doll. This isn't your personal hunting ground. These people come here to relax, not to be__"

"That table over there," Buck interrupted, his eyes locked on Collette, who was laughing at something, her head thrown back, hair cascading over her shoulders. "The group with the blonde. They loo k....out of place."

Jenny followed his gaze and signed. "That's right, they just showed up today. The blond said something about them hiking at Canyon River tomorrow." She narrowed her eyes. "Don't tell me they're your group."

Buck's smile widened. "Two beers, Jenny. One for me and one for...what was your name again?" He smirked at Tim who flushed red.

"Very funny, Buck." Tim mumbled.

"Make it just one beer," Buck corrected, already straightening up to his full height. "Timmy Boy here needs to stay sharp. Someone must carry the gear tomorrow." He grabbed the beer, leaving Tim at the bar.

"Wait...you said I could start off leading the tour tomorrow." Buck smiled back at him as he had already made his way halfway across the room.

Buck approached the table, moving with the confidence of someone who had never been rejected in his life. Samuel noticed him first, his eyes narrowing at the interruption. But Buck's attention was fixed solely on Collette.

"Well, what are the chances?" Buck's voice was smooth as silk. "I couldn't help but notice you folks look like you could use a guide." He pulled up a chair uninvited, turning it backward and straddled it. "I'm Buck, and I'll be leading your adventure tomorrow."

Collette's eyes sparkled with interest as she took in Buck's imposing frame. From the bar, Tim watched his brother work his magic, knowing the outline by heart. Jenny shook her head, sliding Tim a glass of water.

"Trust me, kid" she muttered to Tim, "you don't want to watch this part."

But Tim did watch, as he always did, as Buck commanded the table's attention, making Shannon giggle and Daniel shift uncomfortably closer to her. Even Samuel's dour expression could not dampen Buck's performance. Only Collette genuinely appreciated the show, meeting Buck's intense gaze with one of her own.

"Some people just want to watch the world burn," Jenny sighed, wiping down the bar as Tim slumped forward, knowing tomorrow's trek had just gotten a lot more complicated.

Collette twirled her wine glass, studying Buck with practiced nonchalance. "So, how long have you been playing mountain man?" She leaned back, creating just enough distance to make Buck work for her attention.

"Born and raised in these canyons," Buck replied, his eyes never leaving her face. "Been guiding professionally for eight years now. Though I have to say, none of my previous groups have been quite so..." he paused, letting his gaze linger, "interesting."

"Interesting?" Collette arched an eyebrow. "I hope you're not implying we look out of shape. I hit the gym five times a week." She stretched slightly, knowing exactly how the movement accentuated her figure.

Buck chuckled, deep and resonant. "The trail can be challenging, but I make sure everyone makes it through safely. Four days, three nights under the stars. Nothing builds trust like facing the wilderness together."

"And what about snakes? Bears?" Collette feigned concern, biting her lower lip. "Will you protect us?"

"That's what I'm here for." Buck's smile did not reach his eyes, though no one seemed to notice. "Your safety is my top priority."

Samuel cleared his throat loudly, setting down his scotch. "Is that so?" His lawyer's instincts were kicking in, more from irritation than actual concern. "Tell me, Buck, what exactly are your qualifications? Any certifications we should know about?"

Buck turned toward Samuel, his easy charm never wavering. "Full wilderness first responder certification. Advanced survival training. Member of the California Trail Guides Association." The lies rolled off his tongue smoothly, practiced over countless similar conversations.

"And your safety record?" Samuel pressed, enjoying the chance to cross-examine someone. "Any incidents we should be aware of?"

Tim shifted nervously at the bar, but Buck did not miss a beat. "Not a single serious injury in six years. A few twisted ankles, maybe a blister or two." He winked at Collette. "Nothing I couldn't manage."

"What about insurance?" Samuel continued. "Liability coverage?"

"Full coverage through my company," Buck replied, "But let's not bore these lovely ladies with business talk. Tomorrows about adventure, about pushing boundaries."

Collette nodded enthusiastically. "Exactly! Monica would've hated all this legal talk." She touched Samuel's arm. "She would've wanted us to embrace the experience."

Samuel withdrew his arm, scowling into his drink. The mention of Monica still stung, and watching Collette flirt with this oversized gym rat was not helping.

"Speaking of embracing experiences," Buck leaned closer to Collette, lowering his voice, "the sunset view from Eagle Point is something special. If you are up for a little extra hiking tomorrow..."

From his corner of the bar, Tim watched the familiar scene unfold. He had seen this routine dozens of times – Buck charming his way into their trust, laying the groundwork for what would come later. Tim's stomach churned as he thought about the burner phone in Buck's truck, the one with the contact they would call once they got far enough into the canyon. He pushed the thoughts away, focusing instead on memorizing drink orders. Better to stay useful, to keep Buck happy. After all, what choice did he have?

"Well," Collette stood, smoothing her dress, "I should get some beauty sleep before tomorrow's adventure. Don't want to slow the group down."

"Trust me," Buck replied, standing to his full height, "with me leading the way, you've got nothing to worry about."

If only they knew how wrong, he was.

CHAPTER 8

Purple Prophecy

*T*he river stretched before Samuel, clear and ankle-deep, sunlight dancing across its surface. That is when he saw her—a woman standing mid-stream, her dark hair falling in waves down her back. Something about her silhouette made his heart stop.

"Monica?" His voice echoed against canyon walls he had not noticed before. The woman did not turn, but her shoulders tensed at the sound of his voice. She took a step deeper into the river, water swirling around her calves.

"Wait!" Samuel called out, but his feet felt leaden, refusing to move. "Please, don't—"

The woman paused, and Samuel watched as she slowly lowered her hand into the water. Her fingers spread wide, letting the current thread between them like liquid silk. The gentle flow began to strengthen, tugging at her dress, pulling it downstream.

"Monica, I'm sorry," Samuel whispered, the words he'd never said catching in his throat. The current grew stronger still, water now rushing *past her waist, roaring in his ears. Dark clouds rolled in overhead, casting shadows across the once-clear water.*

The woman started to turn, and Samuel's heart hammered against his ribs. Just before her face came into view, just before he could see if her eyes held the same accusation they had that last morning, just before—

BEEP. BEEP. BEEP.

Samuel bolted upright; his hotel sheets drenched in sweat. The alarm clock's red digits glared 5:00 AM, announcing the start of a day he'd been dreading for weeks. Outside his window, the pre-dawn sky held the same ominous gray as the river's waters.

He pressed his palms against his eyes, trying to erase the image of Monica slipping away, but the sound of rushing water still roared in his ears. Something about the dream felt like a warning, but Samuel pushed the thought aside. He had a hike to get through.

The rideshare van moved its way along the mountain road, each curve bringing them deeper into Canyon Park. Samuel sat rigid in his seat, his expensive hiking boots still pristine and stiff. From the back seat came another burst of giggles—Shannon and Daniel's tenth "private" joke of the morning.

"Oh my god, babe, look at that view!" Shannon pressed her face against the window, her youth and enthusiasm making Samuel's jaw clench. Daniel pulled her closer, whispering something in her ear that made her beam. Samuel watched their reflection in the side mirror, remembering a time when he and Monica had been that naive, that hopeful. Before the failed treatments, before the fights, before—

"Earth to Samuel," Collette's voice cut through his thoughts. She was sitting beside Samuel in the rideshare van, her designer sunglasses perched perfectly on her nose, looking more suited for a Beverly Hills shopping spree than a wilderness trek. "You haven't said a word since we left the hotel."

"Just admiring the local flora and fauna," he replied dryly, glancing back at the young lovers. "Particularly the mating rituals of the young American backpacker."

Collette smirked but kept her eyes on the road. "You know, Buck said this trail has some amazing views. He seems really experienced." Her attempt at casual conversation was not fooling anyone.

"Yes, I'm sure his expertise in tight t-shirts will be invaluable in the wilderness," Samuel muttered.

The van fell quiet except for the soft music playing from Shannon's phone. Samuel watched the landscape change, the civilized world falling away with each mile. Trees grew denser, the air became crisper, and the road narrowed until it felt like they were driving into another world entirely.

"I'm really glad you came, Samuel," Collette said softly, breaking the silence. "It means a lot. You're a good man for doing this for Monica."

Samuel turned to deliver a cutting remark, but something in Collette's voice stopped him. For once, there was no performative grief, no calculated sympathy—just genuine appreciation. He felt his carefully constructed wall crack, just slightly.

"I..." he started, then cleared his throat. "Thank you for organizing this, Collette. Monica always said you were her most loyal friend." The words came out before he could stop them, surprising them both.

Collette reached over and squeezed his hand briefly before returning it to her lap. In the back, Shannon and Daniel had fallen asleep against each other, their young faces peaceful and untroubled.

Samuel turned back to the window, watching the sunlight filter through the trees. This wouldn't be so terrible. There was something to be said for stepping away from depositions and case files, for honoring Monica's memory in a way that didn't involve staring at her empty side of the bed.

The van rounded another bend, and the lodge came into view, a rustic building nestled against the mountainside. In the parking lot, Samuel could make out Buck's imposing figure waiting for them. Standing slightly apart, almost invisible in Buck's shadow, was his brother Tim.

For the first time since Monica's death, Samuel felt something close to peace. He had no way of knowing it would be the last moment of true calm he would feel for a long time.

CHAPTER 9

SAFETY'S SWEET LIES

The main lodge bustled with morning hikers, their excited chatter and boot steps echoing off the vaulted timber ceiling. Sunlight streamed through tall windows, catching dust motes, and making the taxidermic wildlife on the walls cast long shadows. But in the cramped back office, behind the "Staff Only" door, the atmosphere felt heavier, more oppressive.

Tim hunched over the desk, surrounded by filing cabinets and outdated safety posters, his thin frame nearly disappearing into his oversized yellow shirt and blue jeans. "Put that laptop up before Ranger Florence comes in," he muttered, glancing nervously at the door. "You know how she is about procedure."

"Look at this one," Buck's voice boomed, ignoring his brother's concern. "Collette Bennett. Owner of three high-end beauty supply stores." He turned the screen, showing a professional headshot of Collette. "Successful, fit. She'll make the trip interesting."

Tim's long face grew longer. "Maybe we should skip this one. Take a break from guiding for a while."

"A break?" Buck's chair creaked as he leaned back. "Getting tired of our scenic routes, little brother?"

"The trails we use..." Tim ran a hand through his unkempt brown hair. "They're not exactly regulation."

"Since when do you care about regulation?" Buck scrolled through more photos. "Shannon Miller, registered nurse. Daniel Harris, construction worker." His eyes lingered on Collette's image. "Perfect group dynamic."

"The lawyer makes me nervous," Tim said quietly. "Samuel Ross. He seems... thorough."

"Lawyers," Buck scoffed. "They think they can control everything with rules and papers." His massive frame cast a shadow across Tim's desk as he stood. "Nature has different rules, doesn't it, Timmy?"

Tim's shoulders hunched further. "I just think—" "That's your problem," Buck cut him off. "You think too much. Like with Eve. Remember how well that worked out?"

Tim flinched as if physically struck. "That was different."

"Nothing's different. Nothing changes." Buck turned back to the laptop, his voice carrying an edge that made Tim's skin crawl. "You handle the paperwork. I'll plan the route."

Tim stared at his trembling hands, a familiar heaviness settling in his chest. Every trip added weight to whatever was breaking inside him.

"Hey." Buck's voice softened dangerously. "You're not going soft on me, are you? Remember what happens to soft men in this world."

"No," Tim whispered, hatred and fear and resignation warring in his chest. "I'm not soft."

"Good boy." Buck clapped him on the shoulder hard enough to make him wince. "Because this group..." He tapped Collette's photo on the screen. "There's something special about this one."

Tim watched his brother's reflection in the laptop screen, superimposed over Collette's smile. He thought about saying more, about voicing the growing sickness in his gut. But he had learned long ago that resistance only made things worse.

Still, something was different this time. A weariness in his bones, a weight in his chest that felt like change coming. He just did not know if it would be enough to matter.

"Get the safety presentation ready," Buck ordered, already moving toward the door. "And Tim?" He paused. "Don't make me worry about you. You know I hate having to teach you lessons."

Tim nodded, but in his mind, he was counting the cost of his own cowardice. Wondering how many more times he would have to swallow his conscience before something finally broke.

***

The lodge's wooden interior smelled of pine and coffee, its walls decorated with faded trail maps and wildlife warnings. Ranger Florence stood by the projection screen, her red hair pulled back in a practical braid, park badge gleaming. Her warm smile faltered slightly when Buck strutted in behind the group.

"Welcome to Canyon Park, folks," she began, shooting Tim a grin as he struggled with an armload of equipment. "We're going to go through some essential safety protocols before you head out."

"T-these are your emergency packs," Tim stammered, dropping a compass as he approached Shannon. His cheeks flushed as he bent to retrieve it, Buck's divisive snort echoing through the room.

"Smooth moves, Timmy Boy," Buck called out. "Try not to trip over your own feet while you're at it."

Collette stepped forward to help Tim, their fingers brushing as she took her pack. Tim's blush deepened as he mumbled a thank you, quickly averting his eyes from her smile.

"If we're done with the circus act," Ranger Florence interrupted firmly, "let's review the safety video. Tim, would you dim the lights?"

Buck leaned against the back wall, arms crossed over his chest, watching intently as Shannon shifted closer to Daniel during the opening scenes of predator awareness. His eyes gleamed as the video detailed stories of hikers who had gone missing, noting how Collette's manicured fingers tightened around her armrest.

The video droned on with standard safety protocols:

- Always hike in groups of three or more
- Carry emergency locator beacons
- Keep regular radio contact with base camp
- Store food in bear-proof containers
- Know designated emergency shelter locations
- Carry topographical maps and compass
- Monitor weather conditions hourly
- Log all departure and arrival times
- Keep identification and permits visible

"Remember," Ranger Florence added after the video, "cell service is non-existent in most areas. Your guides will have satellite phones for emergencies." She glanced at Buck with barely concealed distrust. "Though I'm sure you won't need them."

Samuel scribbled notes in his phone, his lawyer's instincts kicking in. "What's the protocol if someone gets separated from the group?"

"That won't happen," Buck interrupted smoothly, pushing off the wall. "I never lose a hiker." His smile didn't reach his eyes.

Tim fumbled with the first aid kits, nearly dropping one as he caught Shannon watching him. "We also have emergency r-rendezvous points marked on your maps," he added quietly.

"Which Tim will probably need himself," Buck laughed, causing Ranger Florence to frown.

"Tim's one of our most knowledgeable guides," she corrected sharply. "You're lucky to have him along."

Buck's jaw tightened momentarily before his practiced smile returned. "Of course. My little brother's a regular Boy Scout." He moved closer to the group, standing unnecessarily close to Collette as he began pointing out trail features on the wall map.

Samuel noticed how Tim seemed to shrink under his brother's proximity, how Ranger Florence's hand drifted unconsciously toward her radio when Buck moved through the room. But he was too preoccupied with his own discomfort to register these movements.

Shannon clutched Daniel's arm during the section about mountain lions, while Collette kept her composed facade, though her leg bounced nervously. Buck watched their reactions with barely concealed pleasure, like a cat watching wounded birds.

"Any final questions?" Ranger Florence asked, flicking the lights back on.

"Just one," Buck announced, his voice carrying an undertone that only Tim recognized. "Who's ready for the adventure of a lifetime?"

As the group gathered their gear, Tim caught Ranger Florence's eye. But then Buck's hand clamped down on his shoulder, and the moment passed.

"Remember," Ranger Florence adjusted her badge, maternal concern radiating from her weathered face, "cell service is non-existent in most areas. Your guides will have satellite phones for emergencies."

Her eyes lingered momentarily on Shannon as Daniel helped her adjust her pack. "Though I'm sure you won't need them."

Samuel hung back, something about her tone triggering his lawyer's instinct for detail.

"Ranger Florence? I've been researching Canyon Park's history. .." He watched Tim stiffen slightly at the desk. "There seem to be quite a few incidents over the years. Missing hikers, particularly young women—"

"Oh, those internet theories," Florence chuckled warmly, her red hair catching the morning light.

"Twenty-three years I've served these trails. Every park has its urban legends, especially ones this size."

She patted Samuel's arm like a mother reassuring a worried child. "People see patterns where they want to, especially online."

"But the statistics—" Samuel started.

"Are easily misinterpreted," Florence finished, her ranger persona perfectly calibrated. "Most 'disappearances' are just hikers going off-trail, missing check-in times. They usually turn up at another ranger station, embarrassed and sunburnt." She smiled, the lines around her eyes crinkling. "The canyon just looks more threatening than it is."

At the equipment desk, Tim fumbled with a compass, his eyes darting to Buck who lounged against the wall, watching.

"Tim," Samuel approached, noting how the younger guide's hands shook slightly. "How long have you been leading tours here?"

"F-five years," Tim managed, glancing at Buck. "Maybe six?"

"Any incidents on your tours?"

"Never," Buck cut in smoothly, pushing off the wall. "My brother's too careful. Aren't you, Timmy?"

Florence drifted over to where Shannon was adjusting her hiking poles. "Those are good form," she said softly. "You must work out regularly." Her eyes took in Shannon's athletic build, her short brown hair and wide green eyes, with what seemed like professional appreciation.

"Yoga, mostly," Shannon replied.

"It shows," Florence smiled. "You'll need that flexibility on these trails." She turned to Daniel. "You're lucky to have such a capable partner. Some of these paths require... special handling." Daniel shifted uncomfortably as Florence moved to inspect Collette's pack next.

"Now you," Florence's voice warmed further, "remind me of myself at your age. Such natural poise." She adjusted Collette's pack straps with practiced hands. "The canyon has a way of enhancing natural beauty. Something about the air up there."

Samuel watched these interactions, his unease warring with Florence's calming presence. Her expertise seemed genuine, her concern maternal. Perhaps he was being paranoid, letting internet conspiracies cloud his judgment.

"The most important thing," Florence addressed them all, "is trusting your guides. Buck and Tim know these trails better than anyone." She smiled at Tim, who dropped his gaze.

"Speaking of trails," Buck pushed himself upright, "we should head out while the day's young."

As the group gathered their gear, Florence held Samuel back slightly. "Mr. Ross? Those concerns you found online. They're natural, especially after... well I know your wife was supposed to be on this trip." Her eyes softened with genuine sympathy. "But the canyon isn't the threat. If anything, it is a place of healing. Ask anyone who's walked these trails with an open heart."

Samuel felt his lawyer's skepticism wavering under her maternal gaze. She radiated competence, authority, and most importantly, genuine care. What had he been worried about? "Thanks," he managed, shouldering his pack.

"Stay safe out there," Florence called after them, watching them file out into the morning light. Something flickered behind her eyes – but if anyone had noticed, they might have mistaken it for normal concern about hikers in her care.

The door swung shut behind them, leaving Florence in her domain as they headed toward the trails that would change all their lives forever.

CHAPTER 10

THE PATH BELOW

The morning sun filtered through Canyon Park's dense canopy, casting dappled shadows on the rock-strewn trail. Seventy miles outside Sacramento, the wilderness felt like an entirely different world. Spring had painted the landscape in vibrant greens, and yesterday's rain left everything with a glossy sheen. Droplets fell from overhead branches, creating a gentle percussion that mixed with birdsong and the distant roar of the canyon's river below.

Samuel adjusted his pack for the thousandth time, the straps digging into his shoulders despite his expensive moisture-wicking shirt. The humid air clung to his skin, making him feel like he was swimming rather than hiking. He silently thanked his trainer for pushing him through those grueling HIT sessions, though none of them had prepared him for this form of discomfort.

"The river you're hearing is about eight hundred feet below," Buck announced, his voice carrying effortlessly through the morning air. "We'll be heading down there eventually, but first we're taking the rejuvenation trail." He pointed to a barely visible path that seemed to disappear into the wilderness. "It's less traveled, but the views are worth it."

Tim trailed behind the group, occasionally checking their GPS coordinates with nervous glances at his brother. They had veered off the main trail twenty minutes ago, taking a route that was not marked on any of the official park maps.

"Is this even a maintained trail?" Samuel called out, his leather boots sliding slightly on the wet rocks.

"You're not scared, are you, Lincoln?" Buck smirked over his shoulder. "Thought you city boys loved going off the beaten path."

Collette laughed at Buck's jab, the sound mixing with the rushing water below. She had been walking just behind Buck for the past mile, peppering him with questions about his guiding experience and outdoor adventures. Her hiking pants and fitted jacket looked fresh from REI's window display, but she moved with surprising confidence over the uneven terrain.

"Monica would have loved this," she said, loud enough for Samuel to hear. "Remember how she always wanted to go camping, Samuel?"

The comment struck him like a physical blow. Yes, Monica had wanted to go camping, she had wanted to do a lot of things. But there had always been another case, another client, another round of fertility treatments to schedule.

Shannon and Daniel walked between Samuel and the others, lost in their own world. They stopped every few feet to take selfies or point out interesting plants, their enthusiasm somehow making Samuel feel even more isolated. Their matching backpacks and coordinated hiking outfits mocked him with their carefully planned perfection.

The humidity increased as they descended deeper into the canyon, the air thick enough to chew. Sweat trickled down Samuel's back, and his cotton socks were already damp within his expensive hiking boots. Each step required more concentration as the trail grew less distinct.

"You all getting tired back there?" Buck called out again, his own pack seeming to weigh nothing on his broad shoulders. He'd stopped to help Collette over a fallen log, his hands lingering longer than necessary on her waist. She beamed up at him, and Samuel felt his jaw clench.

"I'm fine," he snapped, watching Collette as she touched Buck's arm in thanks. The gesture reminded him of how Monica used to touch his arm, before everything went wrong, before the arguments about adoption versus IVF, before—

"Watch your step here," Tim's quiet voice interrupted Samuel's thoughts. "The rocks are slippery from the rain."

Samuel nodded curtly, grateful for the practical concern. Tim seemed to be the only one not playing some kind of role on this ridiculous expedition.

Up ahead, Buck was leading them further from the marked trails, away from the occasional glimpses of other hikers they had seen earlier. The river's roar grew louder, more insistent, drowning out the birdsong that had gone with their first steps. Samuel could not shake the feeling that each step took them further from civilization, further from safety.

But then Collette laughed again at something Buck said, the sound echoing off the canyon walls, and Samuel's unease transformed back into irritation. He pushed forward, determined to prove he could handle whatever this trail had to offer. After all, how bad could four days in the wilderness really be?

The answer to that question was still waiting, somewhere ahead on the trail that was quickly becoming no trail at all.

***

A sharp cry pierced the morning air, followed by Shannon's pan-
icked voice yelling "Daniel!"

Daniel had stumbled; his left foot wedged between two slick rocks.
As he tried to catch himself, his ankle twisted with a sickening roll,
sending him sprawling onto the damp ground. His face contorted in
pain as he clutched his ankle.

Shannon dropped beside him, her nurse's instincts overriding her
earlier emotional response. Her hands moved with professional precision, checking for swelling and discoloration. "Don't rotate it," she
commanded, her voice steady despite the concern in her eyes. "The
ligaments could be compromised. We need to check for fractures."

Samuel watched her methodical assessment, with a sudden ache in
his chest. Her gentle efficiency, the way she balanced care with competence – it reminded him so much of Monica with her kindergartners.
Shannon had the same instinct to help, to heal.

"Baby, please let me wrap it," Shannon pleaded, already reaching for
her pack where she kept a basic medical kit. "The anterior ligament
could be—"

"Tim! Buck!" Samuel called out, his voice echoing against the
canyon walls. "We need help back here!"

Buck turned lazily, taking his time to saunter back down the trail.
Tim lingered behind him, shifting his weight nervously from foot to
foot.

"What's the problem, pretty boy?" Buck asked, looking down at Daniel with barely concealed disdain. "Got your designer boots stuck?"

"His ankle rolled," Samuel replied sharply. "It could be sprained."

"I'm fine," Daniel interrupted, his face flushing as he tried to wave off Shannon's concerned hands. Like many young men, Daniel realized, he would rather risk injury than appear weak. How familiar that pride felt.

Buck squatted down, roughly pulling Daniel's boot back and forth. Daniel bit back a yelp, but Shannon's face hardened with outrage.

"Stop that!" she snapped. "You could be causing more damage. You can't just yank on it like that! We need to go back to the lodge and—"

"It's fine," Buck declared, standing, and brushing his hands on his pants. "Just a little twist. Walk it off, man up. Can't let a little ankle slow down the whole group."

Shannon's hands balled into fists. "He needs proper medical attention and rest. The swelling pattern suggests—"

"Listen, princess," Buck's tone carried an edge that made Samuel's lawyer's instincts prickle. "If your boyfriend can't handle a little rough terrain, maybe he should've stayed at the lodge."

Daniel pushed himself up, clearly embarrassed by the attention. "No, it's okay. I'm fine, really." He tested his weight on the ankle, trying to hide his wince. "Buck's right, just need to walk it off."

"You're not fine," Shannon whispered, professional composure cracking. "Please Daniel, let me at least wrap it properly. Look the elevation and terrain will only make it worse."

Samuel stepped forward, his own pattern of dismissing concern suddenly clear in Daniel's stubborn expression. "Maybe we should let Shannon take a look. She knows what she's talking about."

"Yeah, I'm totally fine," Daniel forced a smile, though Samuel noticed how he kept his weight shifted to his right side. Just like Samuel had always pushed through, ignored warnings, dismissed concern until it was too late.

"Well, since we're stopped," Buck announced, "might as well take a bathroom break. I need to drain the dragon." He chuckled at his own crude comment, walking off into the brush. "Tim, hand out some trail mix or something."

Tim fumbled with his pack, distributing bags of mixed nuts and dried fruit with trembling hands. When he reached Shannon, he paused. "I... I have some athletic tape if you want to wrap his ankle," he whispered, glancing nervously in the direction his brother had gone.

Shannon's face lit up with relief. "That would be perfect. The compression could help prevent further—"

"That won't be necessary," Daniel cut her off, still trying to salvage his dignity. "Really, I'm good." He caught her hurt expression and softened his tone. "Babe, I know you're trying to help, but we can't hold everyone up."

Collette sat down next to Shannon, pulling out her water bottle. "You sure you're, okay?" she asked Daniel, but her eyes kept drifting toward the direction Buck had disappeared.

Samuel watched Shannon's shoulders slump in defeat, her medical knowledge warring with her need to respect Daniel's wishes. He recognized that helpless frustration – the pain of watching someone you love refuse help, refuse to acknowledge their own vulnerability.

"The anterior swelling concerns me," Shannon murmured to no one in particular, her fingers fidgeting with her pack's medical supplies. "Without proper support, the repeated impact could—"

"I said I'm fine," Daniel snapped, then immediately looked contrite. "I'm sorry, hon. I just... I can handle it."

Samuel felt an uncomfortable mirror held up to his own past behavior. How many times had Monica tried to tell him something was wrong? How many times had he dismissed her concerns with that same prideful certainty?

The group settled onto various rocks and fallen logs, munching on their snacks in uncomfortable silence. Daniel kept flexing his ankle when he thought no one was looking, while Shannon watched him with the anguish of someone trained to heal forced to watch suffering continue. Tim hovered at the edge of the group, repeatedly checking his watch.

Buck's voice boomed from behind them, making everyone jump. "Alright, ladies and gentlemen, break time's over!" He clapped his hands together. "We've got ground to cover before nightfall. Pretty boy, you good to go, or do you need a piggyback ride?"

Daniel stood quickly, too quickly, as color drained from his face. "Good to go," he said through gritted teeth.

Shannon bit her lip, clearly swallowing back further medical protests. Her hand brushed the medical tape in her pocket – a lifeline she was not allowed to throw.

Samuel caught Tim's eye, noticing how quickly the younger guide looked away. Something wasn't right there, but what could he say? They were already miles from the main trail, and Buck was their only way back.

As they resumed hiking, Samuel made a mental note to keep a closer eye on their guides. But even his sharp legal mind could not have predicted just how important that observation would become, or how soon they'd all wish they'd listened to Shannon's warnings, or how many other warnings they'd missed along the way.

The canyon walls rose around them, indifferent to the human drama unfolding on the trail. But Samuel's perspective had shifted, his own patterns of behavior revealed in Daniel's stubborn pride and Shannon's frustrated concern. Sometimes the hardest injuries to heal were the ones we refused to acknowledge.

CHAPTER 11

LOVES BROKEN SHADOWS

The sun dipped behind the canyon walls, painting the sky in brilliant oranges and purples. The river's constant rush provided a natural soundtrack as the exhausted group reached their camping spot – a relatively flat clearing nestled between the water and the canyon wall. The first stars were beginning to peek through the darkening sky, twinkling like scattered diamonds.

"This is home for tonight, folks," Buck announced, dropping his pack with theatrical flair. "Better get those tents up before it's pitch black."

Tim scanned the ground nervously, kicking aside some brush. "Buck, maybe we should move higher up. This area's known for diamondbacks and water moccasins. Plus, in the ranger guide—"

"Since when are you a snake expert?" Buck cut him off. "The clients always love camping by the water."

Samuel's lawyer instincts prickled. What legitimate guide would dismiss basic safety concerns? And why did Buck keep referring to them as "clients" rather than hikers or campers? Something about their certifications and knowledge seemed oddly mismatched.

"Actually," Samuel interjected, "I looked at the park's guide before we left. It does recommend camping on higher ground, away from—"

"Oh, look who's the outdoor expert now!" Buck's laugh held no humor. "Bet you're real familiar with snakes, being a lawyer and all."

Daniel lowered himself carefully onto a fallen log, trying to mask his grimace. His ankle had swollen noticeably during the day's hike, his boot now uncomfortably tight. Despite his pain, he forced a chuckle at Buck's joke. "He's got you there, Samuel."

Shannon hovered nearby, her earlier enthusiasm replaced by worried glances and barely concealed resentment toward Buck. "Maybe we should listen to Tim. He seems to know these trails."

"Seems to know how to be a chickenshit," Buck muttered. "Collette," he called out louder, as she was holding up tent poles with a practiced smile. "Why don't you let me show you how to set this up properly? Wouldn't want anything collapsing in the middle of the night."

Collette straightened, her expression cooling. "I think I can manage. I've been camping before, you know. Women are capable of basic tasks without male supervision." She turned away, efficiently beginning to unpack her tent, though Samuel noticed her glancing at Buck's reaction from the corner of her eye.

Buck's jaw tightened momentarily before he spun toward Tim. "Hey, genius! Why haven't you started the fire yet? You trying to freeze everyone?"

Tim jumped, nearly dropping the kindling he had been gathering. He cast another nervous glance at the riverside brush where he had spotted movement earlier. "I-I was just collecting—"

"Just collecting excuses," Buck snapped. "Get it done now. Jesus, do I have to think of everything?" He stormed over, snatching the wood from Tim's hands. "Can't you do anything right?"

The group pretended not to notice the exchange, busying themselves with their own tasks. Samuel watched from the corner of his eye as he secured his tent stakes, noting how Tim's hands shook as he arranged the firewood. For someone Buck claimed was an experienced guide, Tim seemed oddly uncertain about basic camping tasks.

A low rumble echoed through the canyon.

"Quiet!" Buck hissed, his hand shooting up. "Nobody move." His eyes scanned the darkening tree line. "Mountain lions! They get bold at dusk."

The group froze. Shannon grabbed Daniel's hand, while Collette stopped mid-tent-stake. Only Tim seemed unconcerned, cocking his head to listen.

"It's just a small plane," Tim said softly.

Tim's correct identification of the plane added to Samuel's unease. The younger guide clearly knew the park's patterns and protocols – so why was Buck, supposedly the senior guide, so dismissive of safety concerns? Something about their dynamic felt rehearsed, like actors playing parts they had performed too many times.

The distinctive sound of a plane engine grew clearer, confirming Tim's assessment. Buck's face darkened as he snatched up a fallen branch and hurled it at his brother, missing him by inches.

"Way to ruin the moment, Tim! Your dumbass is no fun at all." Buck stomped off toward his tent, muttering under his breath.

Collette watched the exchange with growing anger. Once Buck had disappeared into his tent, she approached Tim, who was still trying to start the fire with trembling hands.

"Why do you let him treat you like that?" she asked quietly, kneeling beside him, positioning herself so Buck could see them from his tent.

Tim's eyes darted up, surprised by her presence. His mouth opened and closed several times before he found his voice. "He's... he's not always like this. Sometimes he—"

"He's a bully," Collette interrupted. "You deserve better than that."

Tim's eyes welled with unexpected emotion. Here was this beautiful woman, showing him kindness, seeing him as more than Buck's shadow. For a moment, Tim wanted to tell her everything – about Buck's true nature, about the other trips. His heart raced as he prepared to speak.

But then Buck appeared from his tent, and Tim watched his brother's expression darken at the sight of them together. Pure instinct took over.

"Would you like to take a walk?" Tim blurted, placing his hand awkwardly on Collette's shoulder. "To... to gather more firewood?"

Collette's eyes flicked to Buck, noting his clenched fists and rigid posture. A small smile played at her lips as she stood. "I'd love to," she replied, deliberately loud enough for Buck to hear. "Some men actually know how to treat a woman with respect."

They walked away from the campfire's growing light, leaving Buck to stew in his rejection. Shannon watched them go with a hint of a smile, while Daniel continued to massage his swollen ankle. Samuel saw it all, adding each interaction to his mental notebook of concerns about their guides.

The stars continued to multiply overhead, their cold light reflecting off the river's surface. Samuel watched a water snake slip silently beneath the surface, wondering what other dangers lurked just out of sight. None of them knew it yet, but this peaceful evening was the last moment of normalcy they would experience on this trip.

CHAPTER 12

When Shadows Speak Truth

The forest had grown darker, but enough twilight filtered through the canopy to illuminate their path. Collette watched Tim gather sticks, noting how his shoulders hunched whenever he thought she was looking at him. His nervous energy was palpable, like a wounded animal expecting another blow.

"So, Tim," she began gently, "tell me about yourself. How did you get into being a guide?"

Tim's hands fumbled with a branch. "Grew up around here," he said softly, eyes fixed on the ground. "Dad was an engineer for the state. Smart guy, real smart. Always wanted us to follow in his footsteps."

"Us? You and Buck?"

"Yeah." Tim's voice grew quieter. "Buck was the golden child. Marine Corps, multiple tours in the Middle East. Mom and Dad couldn't have been prouder." He paused, gathering more wood. "I was just... there. The other one."

Collette felt a wave of pity wash over her. "But you found your own path with hiking, right?"

For the first time, Tim's face lit up slightly. "I used to spend every weekend exploring these trails. Knew every bend in the river, every cave, every lookout point. It was my escape, you know? My thing."

"That must have been special."

"Met Eve here," Tim continued, his voice taking on a dreamy quality. "She was a student at Sacramento State, studying biology. We dated for two years. She understood me, understood why I loved these canyons so much."

"What happened?"

Tim's expression darkened. "Buck came home. Eve... she could not resist him. No woman can." His grip tightened on the firewood. "She wasn't good enough anyway. Buck showed me that."

Collette frowned at his words, at how he absolved his brother of any responsibility. "Tim, that wasn't your fault—"

"Were you ever in love?" Tim interrupted abruptly, still not meeting her eyes.

The question caught her off guard. "I... I love my family and my friends. But romantic love? I believe in loving yourself first. Building your own identity before—"

"That's sad," Tim cut in, his voice taking on an unexpected edge. "Really sad. Life without love is not worth living. Eve taught me that. Even though she left, at least I experienced real love."

"That's a rather narrow view," Collette replied, bristling at his judgment. But his words had struck something deep inside her.

Memories of college flooded back – how she had dated Samuel first, three casual months of coffee dates and study sessions. How she had introduced him to Monica at that spring formal, watching their instant connection spark. How she had spent years criticizing his relationship with Monica, picking at their differences, highlighting Samuel's flaws.

Had she been jealous? Not of Samuel specifically, but of their certainty in each other? While she had built her career, her independence, had she been secretly envying their ability to be vulnerable to risk everything for love?

"You're wrong, you know," she said finally. "There are many kinds of love, Tim. Not just—"

But Tim had already started walking back toward camp, leaving her with her unfinished thought. In the growing darkness, his silhouette reminded her of a shadow – formless, undefined, existing only in relation to something else. Or someone else.

She hurried to catch up, her arms full of gathered wood. The river's rush seemed louder now, more insistent, as if trying to warn her of something. But what? Tim's words about love had rattled her more than she wanted to admit, forcing her to confront uncomfortable truths about her relationships, about Monica and Samuel, about herself.

As they approached the campfire's glow, she watched Tim transform – his shoulders hunching further, his steps becoming uncertain, his entire being seeming to shrink as Buck's imposing figure came into view. The brief glimpse she had of his inner world vanished, replaced by the familiar nervous energy of a man desperately seeking approval.

She wanted to reach out, to shake him, to make him see how his brother's influence had warped his view of both love and self-worth. But something in Tim's earlier words gave her pause. There was an intensity to his beliefs about love, a rigidity that felt almost dangerous. Like someone who would do anything, justify anything, in love's name.

Back at the fire, Buck barely acknowledged their return, but his eyes followed Collette's every move as she stored the firewood. She felt the weight of his gaze like a physical thing, heavy with possession and promise. But now, after her conversation with Tim, it carried a new dimension of unease.

The stars had fully appeared, their cold light offering no comfort as the night closed in around them.

CHAPTER 13

WHEN WOLVES CONFESS

The tent zipper rasped open without warning, and Buck's massive frame blocked the entrance. "What's up, Lincoln?" he drawled, ducking inside uninvited twirling a nail in his fingers.

Samuel's lawyer instincts immediately cataloged the invasion - the deliberate dominance play, the dismissive nickname, the violation of personal space. Just like he used to analyze witness behaviors, keeping everything at clinical distance.

"My name's not—" Samuel started.

"Yeah, yeah, like The Lincoln Lawyer, right? Always so serious." Buck wore loose basketball shorts and a white T-shirt that strained across his chest. He flopped onto Samuel's sleeping bag, reaching for Samuel's pack.

"Don't touch that," Samuel snapped, snatching it away. "What do you want?"

"Just trying to make peace, Lincoln." Buck raised his hands in mock surrender. "We got off on the wrong foot." He stretched out, taking up most of the tent's space. "Tell me about Collette. Known her long?"

Samuel shifted uncomfortably, recognizing the predatory interest in Buck's tone.

"We dated briefly in college. She was Monica's sorority sister."

"Ah, sororities," Buck's eyes gleamed. "That was my idea, you know. Marketing these treks to sororities across the country. Best decision we ever made." His tone carried something predatory. "I've always had a way with women. They're all the same really - just need the right handling."

Buck leaned closer, his breath hot in the confined space. "So, did you fuck her? Collette? What was she like?"

Samuel recoiled, not just from Buck's crudeness but from the mirror he was holding up. How many times had he reduced Monica to a function - wife, potential mother, failed IVF participant?

"That's completely inappropriate—"

"Come on, man to man." Buck's smirk widened. "No? Your loss. These educated types - they act all high and mighty, but get them in the right situation..." He made a crude gesture. "They're all the same underneath."

"Tell me about your wife," Buck switched topics abruptly. "Your wife, the one that was supposed to be on this camping trip. What was she like?"

The mention of Monica from Buck's mouth felt like a violation, but something in Samuel softened despite himself. "She was... kind. A kindergarten teacher. Beautiful, inside and out. Much better person than me."

"Show me a picture of her," Buck demanded suddenly.

"I don't have one," Samuel replied.

"Come on, everyone's got pictures on their phone." Buck watched intently as Samuel reached into his backpack's side pouch, pulling out his cell phone.

Samuel hesitated before opening his photos, finding one from their last beach vacation. Monica was laughing, her hair catching the sunset, his arm around her waist. They looked happy. It felt wrong sharing this moment with Buck, but something in his tone made Samuel afraid to refuse.

"Mmm, she's hot, shame she's not here," Buck growled, grabbing his crotch as he leered at the photo. Samuel quickly closed the image, his hand shaking with rage.

Buck leaned back on the sleeping bag. "You know Lincoln, I had some buddies in the Marines eat their guns when we got back," Buck said, his eyes taking on a distant gleam. "Guess they couldn't handle what we did over there. What I did." His chest puffed slightly. "Led my unit in confirmed kills. Battalion record, actually."

The pride in his voice made Samuel's stomach turn. Here was a man who counted human lives like trophies.

"The weak ones couldn't handle it," Buck continued. "But me? I was born for it. Nothing like having that kind of power, Lincoln. Watching the light go out in someone and knowing it's because of you." He grinned, the expression more predatory than human. "Oh...I still get that rush sometimes, you know?" Buck said, putting the nail he was twirling in his fingers in his mouth.

Samuel's legal mind started cataloging red flags, but underneath his analytical approach, a deeper fear grew. This wasn't just toxic masculinity or veteran bravado. This was something darker.

"Of course, civilians don't understand," Buck's voice dropped lower. "They think there's rules, order. Like your courtroom. But out there? In the real world? It's all about power. Who has it, who doesn't." His eyes gleamed. "Who takes it."

"Why do you really do these hikes, Buck?"

Buck stood, adjusting himself lewdly right at Samuel's eye level. "Told you, Lincoln. For the women." He grinned, all teeth and no smile. "Sleep tight, Lincoln."

The tent zipper closed behind him, leaving Samuel alone with the sickening realization that they were miles from civilization with a man who might be more than just a narcissist – he might be a sociopath.

The darkness felt heavier now, filled with implications Samuel's legal mind was racing to process. Buck's casual mention of marketing to sororities, his predatory interest in the women, his complete lack of empathy when discussing violence – it all pointed to something sinister. But what could he do? They were already deep in the canyon, cut off from communication, and Buck knew these trails better than any of them.

Samuel reached for his phone out of habit, but the "No Service" message mocked him in the darkness. He thought about Monica, about how she'd beg him to go camping with her, to step away from his carefully controlled world. Now here he was, in a situation no amount of legal expertise could navigate.

Outside, he heard Buck's low laugh as he passed someone else's tent – Collette's. Samuel's stomach churned. He'd seen plenty of disturbed individuals in his law practice, had cross-examined his share of sociopaths, but they'd always been safely contained within the courthouse walls. Out here, in the wilderness, the rules of civilization felt far away.

The river's constant rush outside suddenly seemed less soothing and more ominous, as if it was ready to swallow any screams that might pierce the night. Samuel didn't know it yet, but sleep would not come easily tonight, or any night left on this trek.

CHAPTER 14

PURPLE DREAMS, DARK WATERS

The river stretched endlessly before Samuel, its waters eerily calm. The woman stood on the opposite shore, her long purple dress billowing in a wind he could not feel. Her back remained turned, dark hair dancing like smoke.

"Monica!" His voice echoed against canyon walls. "Please, look at me!"

She took another step away. Samuel plunged into the river, fighting against the suddenly strengthening current. The water knocked him down, soaking him to the bone. He struggled up, gasping, only to see her figure growing smaller.

"Wait!" He pushed forward again, but the river had other plans. A violent surge pulled him under, the world dissolving into dark water and—

A man's laugh cut through the night, yanking Samuel from his dream. His heart pounding, he unzipped his tent with trembling hands. The cool breeze hit his sweat-dampened t-shirt as he stepped out into the moonlit night.

Drawn by voices near the water, he walked along the shoreline, his bare feet silent on the rocky ground. About fifty feet downstream, a figure appeared from the river like a water nymph. Samuel froze, for a moment thinking his dream had followed him into reality.

But it was Collette, her wet skin gleaming in the moonlight. She stood naked in the shallow water, hands crossed over her breasts, laughing into the night. Samuel felt a guilty heat rise in his chest as he took in her athletic silhouette, water cascading down her curves. His body responded traitorously – six months of grief and celibacy making itself known in an unexpected rush of desire.

The moment shattered as Buck erupted from the water behind her, his massive frame glistening wet, completely naked. He pounded his chest like a gorilla, letting out primal grunts that echoed off the canyon walls. "Who's king of the jungle, baby?"

Collette snatched her shirt from the shore, clutching it to her chest as she darted toward her tent, her laughter trailing behind her. Samuel crouched behind a boulder; his earlier arousal replaced by disgust as Buck flopped back into the water with a thunderous splash.

The scene felt wrong, tainted – like everything about this trip. Buck's visit to his tent earlier, his disturbing questions about Monica, his predatory interest in the women, and now this midnight display of primitive masculinity. It was all too much.

Samuel waited until Buck's splashing faded before creeping back to his tent. His mind was made up. Tomorrow, he would make up some emergency at work, something that required them all to head back early. Shannon and Daniel would be relieved, given Daniel's ankle. Collette might resist, but he would have to make her understand.

As he lay back on his sleeping bag, Samuel thought the woman in purple in his dream had not been Monica, but it was his own conscience, his instinct for survival, walking away from danger. And like the dream, the current was getting stronger, threatening to pull them all under.

He had to get them out of there. Before it was too late.

The river rush seemed to agree, its constant roar now sounding like a warning: Leave. Leave. Leave.

CHAPTER 15

HIGH PLACES BREAK

Dawn crept over the canyon rim, painting the sky pale pink and gold. The morning air carried a chill, and wisps of smoke rose from the fire's dying embers. Shannon and Daniel huddled close together by the fire pit, both looking drawn and tired. Daniel's ankle had swollen noticeably overnight, and Shannon kept shooting worried glances at Buck's tent.

Samuel approached them, his own sleepless night clear in his face. "How's the ankle?" he asked quietly, crouching beside them.

"It's been better," Daniel grimaced, shifting his weight. "I didn't sleep much."

Samuel glanced around to ensure Buck and Tim were not within earshot. "Listen, I need to head back to the hotel today. I forgot to file a crucial document for a case and there could be serious consequences if I don't get it done today." He paused, watching their reactions. "And honestly, Daniel, that ankle needs proper medical attention."

Shannon's shoulders relaxed slightly, as if she had been waiting for an excuse to leave. "I was thinking the same thing about his ankle. But Collette..." she trailed off, looking toward her friend's tent.

"Something's not right here," Samuel continued, lowering his voice further. "I don't trust Buck. Or Tim, for that matter. Their credentials, their behavior – it all feels off."

"Yeah, and the way Buck treated Daniel's injury," Shannon agreed, her voice barely above a whisper. "No professional guide would be so dismissive. And the way he looks at us sometimes..." She shuddered slightly.

"Last night," Daniel started, then hesitated. "I think I heard things. Voices by the river. Laughter that didn't sound... right."

Samuel nodded grimly. "We need to leave. All of us. Today."

"We're in," Shannon said quickly, squeezing Daniel's hand. "But Collette won't be easy to convince. She's... fascinated by Buck."

Samuel stood, steeling himself for the harder conversation ahead. Collette was doing yoga on a flat rock near her tent, her face glowing with an enthusiasm that made his stomach turn. She barely acknowledged him as he approached.

"Collette, we need to talk."

"Oh, Samuel it's a beautiful morning, isn't it?" she replied, transitioning into another pose. "The air feels so alive up here."

"I have bad news; I need to head back today. I have an urgent case—"

"Bullshit." Collette dropped her pose, fixing him with a hard stare. "You've been looking for an excuse to leave since we got here. Monica would be so disappointed—"

"Don't." Samuel's voice turned sharp. "Don't use her name to justify staying here. Buck is dangerous."

Collette laughed, but it held no humor. "Dangerous? Because he is confident? Because he makes you feel insecure?"

"No, that hulk reject doesn't make me feel insecure. Listen he came to my tent last night," Samuel pressed on. "He flopped on my air mattress and started asking about Monica, about her suicide. Then he got off by it. He grabbed himself while looking at Monica's picture, Collette. The man's a predator."

"Oh my God, Samuel," Collette exploded, standing up. "You can't stand that I might be interested in someone! You have always been like this – controlling, judgmental. Even in college, before Monica—"

"Jesus Collette, this isn't about us!" Samuel pleaded. "There is something seriously wrong here. The way they market to sororities, Buck's military stories, his brother's strange behavior. We need to leave. Now."

"You want to know what this is really about?" Collette stepped closer, her voice dripping with venom. "You're guilty. Guilty about Monica, about the IVF, about everything. And now you are seeing dangers everywhere because it is easier than facing yourself!"

"Everything okay over here?"

They both turned to find Buck approaching, his massive frame blocking the morning sun. He was already dressed and ready to continue the hike with his easy smile not reaching his eyes.

"Perfect timing," Collette said brightly, though her voice trembled slightly. "Samuel here was just leaving. Something about needing to go back to work on a case or something."

Buck's smile widened, showing too many teeth. "Leaving? That's not possible, Lincoln. We are miles from any marked trail. Could be dangerous, trying to find your way back alone."

"Well then I guess we all go," Samuel said firmly, meeting Buck's gaze. "Daniel's ankle needs medical attention."

"The pretty boy's fine," Buck dismissed. "Besides, you signed waivers. Cannot deviate from the planned route without assuming full liability. You're a lawyer – you understand liability, don't you?"

Samuel felt the trap closing. Any waivers they had signed were meaningless if Buck and Tim were not licensed guides, but proving that out here, miles from civilization, wouldn't help them.

"See?" Collette said triumphantly. "It's settled then. We stick to the plan." She turned to Buck with an adoring smile. "Where are we heading today?"

"Got a special spot picked out," Buck replied, his eyes never leaving Samuel's face. "It's really private. No other hikers ever go there." His grin turned predatory. "You're gonna love it, Lincoln."

Samuel watched helplessly as Collette followed Buck back toward the main camp, her body language all but screaming her attraction to him. Sitting next to the dead fire, Shannon and Daniel wore matching expressions of concern.

The morning birds had gone quiet, as if they too sensed the shift in the air. Samuel looked toward the river, remembering his dream, the woman in purple walking away. But this time, there would be no waking up from the nightmare they were walking into.

He had tried to warn them. Now all he could do was watch and wait for whatever Buck had planned for their "special spot."

CHAPTER 16

THE PERFECT SHOT

The trail wrapped upward like a serpent, each step steeper than the last. Samuel's calves burned as he trudged behind the group, watching Buck lead them higher and higher into the canyon's embrace. The morning sun had grown fierce, and Samuel's shirt clung to his back with sweat.

"How much further?" Daniel called out, his limp more pronounced on the incline.

"Almost there, princess," Buck shouted back. "Quit your whining."

The river below had transformed from the wide, rushing body they had camped beside into a silver thread weaving through the landscape. Samuel felt his stomach lurch each time he looked down – they must have climbed at least 700 feet already. The height made him dizzy, but something else nagged at his consciousness: they were getting further from any help.

Collette practically bounced up the trail ahead of him, her ponytail swinging with each step. "This is exhilarating!" she called back.

"Samuel, isn't this amazing?" Her enthusiasm felt like a personal rebuke of his earlier warnings.

Shannon helped Daniel navigate a particularly steep section, while Tim brought up the rear, constantly checking his backpack as if ensuring something precious remained inside. The gesture made Samuel uneasy, but the thin air and exhaustion had begun to dull his sharp edges.

"Here we are!" Buck's voice boomed from above. "Welcome to Eagle Point!"

They appeared onto a natural platform of rock, dotted with a few stubborn trees that had somehow taken root in the stone. The view stole what little breath Samuel had left. The entire canyon spread before them like a living map – verdant fields stretching to the horizon, the river cutting through them like a silver knife. Morning haze had burned away, leaving the world clear and somehow softer from this height.

"Oh my God," Collette breathed, stepping closer to the edge. "It's beautiful."

Behind them, Tim fumbled in his backpack, producing a professional-looking camera and a small leather pouch that he quickly stuffed in his pocket. His hands trembled as he checked the camera's settings.

"Well, was it worth the climb now, Lincoln?" Buck's voice carried a note of triumph as he clapped Samuel's shoulder hard enough to make him stumble. "And think you wanted to leave. You would have missed all this."

Samuel had to admit, grudgingly, that the view was spectacular. Up here, the river's constant roar that had haunted his dreams had faded to silence, replaced by the pure, clean whisper of wind. For the first time since the trip began, he felt something close to peace. Maybe he had been paranoid.

Maybe—

"Alright, everybody gather 'round," Buck commanded. "It's time to take the money shot. Tim, get that camera ready."

"Group photo time!" Collette positioned herself near the edge where the view was most dramatic. Shannon helped Daniel hobble into place beside her.

"Little closer to the edge," Buck directed, using his bulk to herd them toward the precipice. "We need to get that backdrop just right."

Samuel moved to join them, but something made him hesitate. The leather pouch in Tim's pocket. The way Buck's eyes gleamed as he positioned the group. The subtle shift in Tim's stance as he raised the camera.

"Samuel, come on!" Collette waved him over. "Don't be a spoil-sport."

The wind whispered through the sparse trees, and for a moment, Samuel thought he heard Monica's voice in it – a warning? A farewell? The peaceful feeling began to curdle in his stomach.

"That's it, perfect," Buck said, stepping back to survey the scene. "Tim, make sure you get this right. We want to remember this moment forever."

Samuel watched Tim's hands shake as he adjusted the camera. Buck's stance widen slightly, like a predator preparing to pounce. Buck watched the oblivious smiles on Collette and Shannon's faces as they posed at the edge of the world.

The river might have been silent from this height, but in Samuel's mind, it screamed a warning. This was not about capturing a memory. This was about creating one – one that would explain whatever was about to happen next.

But before he could voice his revelation, before he could shout a warning, Buck's voice rang out:

"Say cheese, everyone!"

And in that moment, suspended between the sky and earth, between warning and action, between safety and catastrophe, Samuel realized why Buck had chosen this spot. Why he had called it special. Why he had wanted them all at the edge.

The wind picked up, carrying with it the sound of destiny about to unfold.

***

"Ladies together, guys together!" Buck commanded, orchestrating the group like a twisted choreographer. "Tim, why don't you stand with the girls? Make sure they're positioned just right."

Samuel felt a flicker of annoyance at the arbitrary shuffling but moved next to Daniel, who was still favoring his uninjured ankle. The wind whipped around them, tugging at their clothes, as if trying to pull them back from the edge.

Tim approached Collette and Shannon, his hands trembling as they disappeared into the leather pouch. The syringes felt heavy, loaded with enough ketamine to drop both women in seconds. His breath came in short bursts as he positioned himself behind them.

"Perfect," Buck's voice carried an edge Samuel had never heard before. "Everyone smile."

Time fractured into crystalline moments:

The metallic whisper of Buck's hand sliding behind his back.

The glint of sunlight on the silencer.

The soft 'pfft' that seemed impossibly quiet for something so devastating.

Daniel's body jerked, a small round hole appearing in his temple like a third eye. His knees buckled, folding him to the ground like a marionette with cut strings. Blood bloomed around him like a crimson halo.

Samuel's world tilted on its axis. He looked down at Daniel's crumpled form, watching red seep into the gray rock. His mind refused to process what his eyes were seeing.

Another soft 'pfft.'

White-hot pain exploded across Samuel's face as the bullet carved a burning path through his flesh. He staggered backward, his heel meeting empty air where solid ground should have been. Behind him, infinity waited.

As he began to fall, time slowed to a grotesque crawl. He saw Collette's eyes go wide as Tim's needle found her neck. Watched Shannon's mouth open in a scream that never came as the second syringe plunged into her shoulder. Their bodies began to sag as the ketamine raced through their veins.

Samuel reached for them, his fingers grasping only air. The sky and earth traded places as he pitched backward into nothingness. The cliff face rushed past him – rock, dirt, scrub brush, rock again. Each impact sent shockwaves through his body. Something cracked in his chest. His shoulder exploded in agony.

He tumbled through space, the world spinning in nauseating circles. Sharp rocks tore at his clothes, his skin, his flesh. The taste of copper filled his mouth. Still, he fell.

A larger rock caught his head with a sickening crack. Colors burst behind his eyes – red, white, purple like Monica's dress. The canyon walls blurred. The roar of wind in his ears began to fade.

His last conscious thought was of Monica, standing in the river of his dreams. She was not walking away this time. She was reaching for him.

Then darkness swallowed everything.

Above, on Eagle's Point, Buck holstered his weapon and surveyed the scene with cold satisfaction. Daniel's lifeless body was cooling on the rocks. Blood marking where Samuel had stood before his fall. Tim carefully lowering the unconscious women to the ground, their faces peaceful as if in sleep.

"Get the zip ties," Buck ordered, already reaching for his satellite phone. "We need to move fast." Buck reached in for his burner phone and tossed it to Tim. "Tell them we have two fresh ones." Buck kicked a loose stone over the edge, listening to it clatter down the cliff face where Samuel had disappeared. "He's toast. Too easy. No way he survived that fall, even if I missed the shot."

Tim's hands shook as he bound the women's wrists, trying not to look at Daniel's body or the empty space where Samuel had been. The wind caught his brother's cruel laughter and carried it out over the canyon, where it echoed like a promise of horrors yet to come.

The river churned below, ready to accept whatever secrets the canyon chose to keep.

CHAPTER 17

Broken Body, Rising Soul

The darkness swirled, and suddenly Samuel was back in his home office, six months after the miscarriage. Monica stood in the doorway, clutching the IVF clinic brochures, her eyes bright with desperate hope.

"They have a new protocol," her voice trembled. "With much better success rates. Dr. Chen says with my hormone levels—"

"Monica...we've been through this," Samuel did not look up from his briefs. "The Thompson merger is at a critical phase. We need to be strategic about timing."

"Strategic?" Monica's voice cracked. "Our baby died, Samuel. Our daughter. This isn't about timing or strategy—"

"That's exactly what this is about," he finally looked up, his tone lawyer sharp. "You're still emotional Monica. You're not thinking clearly. The odds of success at your age—"

"Emotional?" She stepped into the room. "Of course I'm emotional! I held her inside me. I named her. While you... you were back at work three days later like nothing happened."

Samuel stood, straightening his tie. "Someone had to maintain per-spective. Keep things running while you—" "

While I what? Grieved our child? Like a normal human being?" She thrust the brochures toward him. "Just look at the information. Please Samuel."

Instead, he took the papers and deliberately dropped them in the trash. "This discussion is over. We'll revisit when you're thinking rationally."

Monica's face crumpled, but he was already looking back at his computer screen. He never saw how she pressed her hand against her heart, like she was trying to keep something from breaking.

"You're drowning me," she whispered, but he was already lost in case law...

Samuel returned to consciousness in stages. First came the pain – sharp, insistent, but somehow distant, as if belonging to someone else. Then sound: water rushing somewhere nearby, birds calling overhead. Finally, light pierced his closed eyelids, demanding attention with cruel persistence.

He opened his eyes slowly, squinting against the harsh sunlight. The canyon wall stretched above him like a tombstone, its red-brown face indifferent to his suffering. Memories crashed back in devastating waves: Daniel's lifeless body crumpling, the bullet's heat searing across grazing his face as he turned his head, Collette and Shannon's bodies going limp as Tim stuck them with those syringes. Each image hit him like a physical blow, threatening to overwhelm his already fragile consciousness.

Taking inventory of his injuries, Samuel moved each limb carefully, like a crash victim testing for survival. His left shoulder screamed in protest – the dislocated joint sickeningly when he tried to move it. Three or four ribs shifted unnaturally when he breathed, sending lightning bolts of pain through his chest. His head throbbed where it had struck the rock, and dried blood matted his hair in sticky clumps. His right ankle was swollen but could bear weight. Cuts and bruises decorated his body like a brutal abstract painting, each one telling its own story of the fall.

"Lucky," he muttered, tasting blood from a split lip. The scattered brush and smaller rock outcroppings had broken his fall enough to prevent fatal injury. He should be dead. Like Daniel. The thought came unbidden, unavoidable.

Daniel. The image of that small, neat hole in his temple made Samuel retch, bringing up nothing but bile. The young man's final expression of surprise haunted him – another life he did not protect, another death he had seen helplessly.

His backpack lay a few feet away, torn but intact. Samuel crawled to it, each movement sending fresh waves of pain through his chest. He noticed his water bottle was crushed but still had liquid. First aid kit. Trail mix. Map. Samuel rifled through his pockets with increasing desperation.

No phone. The realization hit him like another fall. Buck's visit to his tent, asking to see Monica's picture – he had watched Samuel pull the phone from that specific pocket. Buck had planned this all along. The bastard had been playing them from the start.

His first coherent thought was to get out, find help. The lawyer's mind kicked in: he had evidence of attempted murder. He could bring the whole operation down with proper authorities. It was a logical choice. The smart choice.

He pushed himself up, orienting toward the park's entrance. Every legal and survival instinct screamed to retreat, to save himself. His injuries needed medical attention. The odds of him, alone and wounded, successfully rescuing two women from armed traffickers were astronomically low.

Three steps toward safety, Monica's voice whispered in his mind: "You're drowning me."

Samuel froze. How many times had he chosen the safe path? The logical route? How many times had he calculated odds while someone he loved slipped beneath the surface?

He looked back toward the canyon depths where Collette and Shannon had disappeared. His analytical mind presented the facts: he was injured, outnumbered, unarmed. The smart play was to get help.

But Monica's face floated before him – not from the happy beach photo Buck had leered at, but from that day in his office. The day he had thrown away hope along with those brochures. The day he had chosen logic over love once again.

"I can't walk away again," he said aloud, his voice rough. "Not this time."

The lawyer in him continued arguing they'd need vehicle access, would stick to certain routes. He could deduce their path. But for the first time in his life, Samuel wasn't interested in building a case. He was ready to render judgment.

He turned back toward the canyon's heart, every step sending pain through his battered body. But he welcomed it now. The pain meant he was alive. The pain meant he could still act. Still make a difference.

Samuel's legal mind kicked in, analyzing the situation with desperate clarity:

1. Buck and Tim were professionals. The sorority marketing, the remote location, the precise execution – they had done this before.

2. They needed Collette and Shannon alive, or they would have shot them like Daniel.

3. Tim's syringes meant they needed them unconscious but unharmed.

4. They'd have to transport them somewhere.

5. Was the entire operation using Canyon Park as a cover?

But even as he formed the plan, shame burned in his chest. Running away. Again. Always choosing the pragmatic path, always calculating odds instead of acting on instinct. Wasn't that what had driven Monica to that bathtub?

Her voice whispered in his mind: "Always the pragmatic one, aren't you?"

"I can't walk away again," he said aloud, his voice rough with emotion and dehydration. "Not this time."

The smart choice would be to retreat, to save himself. His injuries screamed for medical attention. Every legal instinct, every survival instinct urged him to turn back.

But Monica's words echoed: Sometimes you must act from your heart.

Samuel forced himself to stand, fighting through waves of dizziness. He studied the canyon walls, noting where the sun hit them. East. They would have to head east with the women – the main road lay that way, and they would need vehicle access for transport.

The lawyer in him continued building the case, unable to completely silence his analytical nature:

- They wouldn't take main trails
- They'd need a rendezvous point accessible by vehicle
- Time would be critical – they couldn't risk discovery
- They'd have planned their route carefully

Samuel pulled out the map with his good hand, spreading it against a rock. His eyes traced routes, looking for service roads or fire breaks that could accommodate vehicles while staying hidden from regular park traffic.

There – an old logging road, marked as decommissioned, that cut through the eastern canyon. Remote enough for privacy, stable enough for vehicles. If he were planning a trafficking operation, that is where he would coordinate exchanges.

Samuel repacked his bag, keeping only the essentials to stay light. His dislocated shoulder would slow him down, but he had managed worse pain in HIT. His broken ribs would also be a problem if he had to fight, but first he had to find them.

He took a small sip of water, rationing it carefully. Looking up at the canyon rim where Daniel's body had once laid cooling in the sun, Samuel felt something fundamental shift inside him. The calculating, cautious lawyer who always weighed odds and considered consequences faded away. In his place stood a man with nothing left to lose – and, finally, something worth fighting for.

"I'm coming for them," he promised the empty canyon. Whether he was talking to Buck and Tim, or to Monica's ghost, he was not sure.

Samuel's split lip curved into a grim smile as he thought of Buck's smugness, his certainty. The hulk like bastard had no idea what guilt and grief could drive a man to do. No idea how liberating it felt to finally stop calculating odds and start following his heart.

He had to hurry. Time was running out, and the canyon held darker secrets than he had imagined. But for the first time since Monica's death, Samuel felt truly alive. The pain, the fear, the determination – it all meant something now.

It meant redemption.

CHAPTER 18

RADIO STATIC SECRETS

Buck laughed softly, nudging Daniel's lifeless body with his boot. "Clean shot, wasn't it? Right through his pretty boy head." He turned to Tim, who was staring at the blood seeping into the rock. "What's wrong, Timmy? Getting squeamish?"

"I'm done," Tim whispered, his hands trembling. "No more, Buck. The killing, the girls... I can't—"

"Can't what?" Buck's amusement vanished. "Can't handle it? Just like you couldn't handle Eve?"

Tim's head snapped up, color draining from his face. "Don't... don't talk about her."

"Why not? Sweet little Eve, thinking you were her knight in shining armor." Buck's smile turned cruel. "Remember how she looked at you? Like you mattered? Before she learned what a pathetic excuse for a man you really are."

"Shut up." Tim's voice cracked.

"She came to me, you know. Begging for a real man's attention." Buck moved closer, towering over his brother. "Just like they all do.

Because that's all you're good for, little brother – warming them up for me."

Tim lunged forward, fists clenched, but Buck didn't even flinch. They both knew it was an empty gesture.

"There he is!" Buck laughed. "Finally showing some spine! But we both know you won't do it. You can't. You're nothing without me, Timmy. Who else would want you?"

Tim's shoulders slumped, the fight draining from him. His eyes drifted to Shannon and Collette's unconscious forms.

"That's right," Buck's voice softened mockingly. "Go tend to your sleeping beauties. It's what you're good at – playing nurse while real men handle business." He patted Tim's cheek. "Good boy."

Tim turned away, kneeling beside the women to check their vital signs. His gentle movements contrasted sharply with the tears sliding down his face.

"Get them ready to move," Buck ordered, pulling out his satellite phone. "T's waiting, and these two will fetch a nice price." He paused, watching Tim arrange the women's limbs with careful precision. "Just remember, brother – you're in this as deep as we are. No going back now."

Tim nodded numbly, but something had shifted in his eyes. The same look he'd had after Eve – the look of a man realizing exactly what he'd become and wondering if there was still a path to redemption.

Buck turned away to make his call on the satellite radio, already dismissing his brother's momentary rebellion. He didn't notice how Tim's hands lingered protectively over Shannon and Collette, or how his gaze drifted to the canyon's edge where Samuel had fallen. Sometimes the biggest changes start with the smallest acts of defiance. Buck held the satellite radio in his hand, his muscled frame casting a long shadow over Tim as he watched his younger brother fuss over the

unconscious women. Where Buck was all hard angles and brutal efficiency, Tim's smaller frame moved with gentle precision, carefully
arranging their limbs in recovery positions, checking pulses for the
third time with trembling fingers.

They had always been opposite sides of the same coin – Buck
built like their father, six-foot-four of military-hardened muscle and
cruel confidence, while Tim took after their mother's side, five-ten
and lean, better suited for climbing trees than breaking necks. But the
real difference lay in their eyes – Buck's cold and calculating, Tim's
haunted by every face they'd ever "guided" through these canyons.

"Would you quit playing nurse and help me get them ready for
transport?" Buck snapped, biceps flexing as he hefted his pack. Tim
kept adjusting Shannon's head, ensuring her airway remained clear,
his touch almost reverent.

"The dosage has to wear off naturally," Tim mumbled, brushing
Collette's hair from her face. "We can't risk complications." Like the
girl that previous time, whose vacant eyes still visited his nightmares.

Buck rolled his eyes as he keyed the radio, his movements precise
and practiced. "T, this is Buck. We have the assets. Clean acquisi-
tion." He glanced at Daniel's cooling body with the same interest he
might show a broken branch. "Minor disposal required. One witness
eliminated, one self-eliminated." He smirked, remembering Samuel's
backwards tumble into space.

Tim's hands began to shake harder. Years of suppressed guilt bub-
bled up like poison. "I can't... I can't do this anymore."

Buck turned slowly, his shadow engulfing his brother. "What did
you say?"

"These women – they're people." Tim stood, though his height still
left him looking up at Buck. "They have families, lives. Like all the
others we've..." His voice cracked. "I want out."

Buck's laugh was as hard as his fists. "Out? To what? Look at yourself, little brother. Weak. Soft. What would you do without me? Without this family?"

The radio crackled. "Confirmed. Status of assets?" T's voice was all business, no hint of concern or remorse, no sign of any warmth.

"Prime condition. Two females, early thirties, and late twenties. Blonde and brunette. Physical fitness level high. No visible markings or complications." Buck rattled off the details like reading a grocery list, his Marine training evident in every clipped syllable. "Premium merchandise."

Tim winced at the clinical description, remembering how he had once helped a girl in this canyon over two years ago – he had slipped her water and loosened her restraints. Buck had found out. The girl was still taken as scheduled, and Tim had spent three days unable to open his swollen eyes from Bucks wrath.

"Proceed to rendezvous point alpha by nightfall," T responded. "Buyers are already in route. Don't be late."

"Copy that." Buck pocketed the radio and stalked toward Tim; muscles coiled like a predator. "Get your shit together. We need to move."

Tim was checking their pupils again, his gentle touch a stark contrast to Buck's looming menace. "Shannon's breathing is slightly shallow. I should reduce the next dose—"

"Jesus Christ!" Buck grabbed Tim's collar, easily lifting his smaller frame. "They're products, not patients. Get your head straight or I'll leave you up here with the pretty boy." He jerked his head toward Daniel's body.

Tim's face crumpled. "I just don't want to damage—"

"Oh, so you don't want to damage them. Try explaining to the buyers why we are late dumbass. Buck released him, sending Tim stumbling. "Now get your pack on. We're double-timing it to the rendezvous."

Tim nodded quickly, tears threatening. Where Buck moved with military precision, Tim's movements were almost choreographed, carefully wrapping each woman in emergency blankets to protect them from scratches. He whispered apologies as he worked, earning a disgusted look from his brother.

"I'll take the blonde," Buck announced, hoisting Collette over his shoulder in a fireman's carry, his muscles flexing for no one's benefit. "She's been making eyes at me anyway. Shame she won't remember our midnight swim."

Tim struggled with Shannon's weight, arranging her as gently as possible across his smaller frame. Every woman they had taken seemed to get heavier, as if his guilt added pounds to their undo.

CHAPTER 19

A Lawyer's Last Defense

The afternoon sun beat down mercilessly as Samuel scanned the canyon floor for anything he could use as a weapon. His HIT trainer's JP's voice echoed in his mind: "Control your breathing. Pain is just weakness leaving the body." He'd scoffed at those platitudes during workouts, but now they felt like survival mantras.

A fallen branch caught his eye – oak, sturdy enough to support weight but light enough to swing. His dislocated shoulder screamed as he worked it free from the underbrush. The lawyer in him appreciated the irony: his first real weapon was a stick, far from the polished mahogany of his courtroom podium.

A sound echoed off the canyon walls – a wildcat's cry, impossible to pinpoint. Samuel's breath hitched, but he forced himself to regulate it like during hill sprints. Four counts in through the nose, four counts out through the mouth. The pain wasn't going away, but he could choose how to respond to it.

The heat pressed down like a physical weight; the air so thick it felt like breathing through wet cotton. Sweat soaked his torn shirt, stinging the cuts scattered across his torso. Each step required conscious thought – the kind of measured suffering he'd endured during HIT competitions, but with actual lives at stake.

He tested the stick's balance, remembering the traditional martial arts classes Monica had wanted them to take together. "It would be good for us," she'd said. "Something we could learn as a team." He'd been too busy preparing for the Thompson merger to even consider it.

Another wildcat cried, closer this time. Samuel gripped his makeshift staff tighter, noting how his tactical thinking was already shifting. The branch wasn't just a walking aid anymore – it was a potential weapon, a tool for survival. Like his body, transformed from courtroom accessory to warrior's instrument through years of training he'd never expected to use like this.

The canyon stretched endlessly ahead, red rocks shimmering in the heat haze. Samuel focused on his breathing again, compartmentalizing pain like he organized case files. Shoulder: manageable if immobilized. Ribs: painful but functional. Head wound: concerning but not debilitating. Each injury cataloged and filed away, leaving room to focus on the mission.

Movement caught his eye – a snake slithering under a rock, seeking shade. The wilderness was teaching him new laws: survival, adaptation, transformation. No judge would sustain objections out here. No legal precedent would protect him from the elements or predators – human or otherwise.

He paused in a patch of shade, the brief respite highlighting how his expensive moisture-wicking shirt had failed in its primary purpose. Monica would have known how to handle this environment. She'd grown up hiking these canyons with her father, while Samuel had grown up in air-conditioned libraries preparing for a life of legal combat.

The irony wasn't lost on him – he'd spent years building his body into a weapon through HIT, but always for show, for control. Now that same training might mean the difference between life and death. Between saving Collette and Shannon or failing them like he'd failed Monica.

A distant rumble of water reached his ears. The river lay ahead – another obstacle, another test. Samuel adjusted his grip on the branch, feeling calluses form where smooth palms once shook clients' hands. Out here, beyond the reach of civil law, he was becoming something else. Something forged in heat, pain, and determination.

The wildcat screamed again, but this time Samuel didn't flinch. He was no longer prey. The predators awaiting him weren't big cats, but something far more dangerous. And he was done running from threats. Pain had become his companion now, keeping him sharp, keeping him focused. The canyon air filled his lungs, carrying the scent of sage and sunbaked stone. A red-tailed hawk circled overhead, hoping Samuels stumbling progress would end in its favor.

His legal training had taught him to build cases in detail, and now he pieced together their trail like a brutal evidence chain. Samuel looked up and noticed broken twigs too high for a mountain lion. He saw scuff marks on rocks where heavy loads had scraped past. He then saw over in a bush a discarded wrapper from medical supplies – He figured that had to belong to Tim and Buck. Tim's careful preparation had betrayed their path. Samuel figured they were carrying unconscious women, which meant they would leave signs no matter how careful they were.

A rattlesnake's warning buzz froze Samuel and forced him to backtrack, precious minutes lost finding another route. The detour led him through a dense patch of thorny brush that left his exposed skin looking like an abstract painting in red.

The river curved ahead, growing wider and more insistent. Its roar mocked his hesitation as he consulted his map, gritting his teeth as he moved his injured arm. The old logging road lay on the other side – they would have to cross somewhere. Which meant Buck and Tim would need to find a manageable point with their unconscious cargo.

"Think like them," he muttered, scanning the riverbank where clusters of cottonwoods dipped their roots into the current. "Can't risk dropping them. Can't risk getting the trucks stuck. They've done this before..."

A quarter mile downstream, the river widened and flattened, creating a natural crossing point. Ancient tire tracks, almost worn away, still scarred the banks. Recent disturbances in the gravel showed where multiple feet had passed. This was it.

Samuel approached the water's edge, his lawyer's mind calculating risks and probabilities. The current looked manageable, the depth chest-high at most. But with one working arm and a broken rib what were the odds of crossing safely...

Monica's voice floated through his mind: "Sometimes you have to stop thinking and just move."

He stripped off his torn shirt, using it to bind his injured arm close to his chest – a makeshift immobilizer. His backpack would get soaked, but he needed the supplies. The water felt like ice when he stepped in, stealing his breath and sending shock waves through his injuries. He was grateful for his cold plunge training. That cold plunge tub on the back porch of his townhome in Atlanta had prepared him for extreme cold temperatures.

"Keep moving," he commanded himself, pushing deeper into the current. The smooth river rocks shifted treacherously under his feet.

A water snake slithered past, adding a spike of primal fear to his cocktail of pain and determination. Halfway across, the water reached his chest, and his feet briefly lost contact with the bottom. His ribs screamed as he fought to stay upright.

For a moment, he was back in his dream – the current trying to pull him under as Monica was walking away. But this time, he wasn't sleeping. This time, he had a purpose.

His right knee struck a submerged rock hard, sending a bolt of agony up his leg. He felt something tear; something give way. The current seized its advantage, pulling at him with greedy fingers. Samuel thrashed, his good arm sweeping through the water as his head went under. The cold shocked his system, making him gasp and swallow river water.

Your HIT endurance won't mean shit if you drown, the lawyer in him noted coldly.

Samuel's flailing hand found a submerged log, and he pulled himself up, coughing and spitting. Three more steps, each one sending lightning through his damaged knee. Two more, the current spinning him like a top. Then suddenly he was dragging himself onto the opposite bank, shivering and gasping but alive. He allowed himself thirty seconds to rest, no more, though his knee throbbed with a deep, warning pain.

The tracking was easier on this side – two sets of boots, bearing extra weight, heading east toward the logging road. Broken branches at shoulder height showed where they had passed with their burdens. They were not even trying to hide their trail now. Why would they? The only witnesses were dead or soon to be sold.

Samuel's wet clothes clung to him as he moved through the undergrowth, but he ignored the discomfort. A family of deer burst from the trees ahead of him, startling him into a defensive crouch that made every injury sing. The terrain started to slope upward, leading to a ridge that would connect with the logging road. They would be moving slower carrying Collette and Shannon, especially Tim. If he pushed hard, despite his new limp, he might have a chance to catch them.

Near a withered juniper, he found a scrap of emergency blanket snagged on a branch – silver, metallic, like the ones he had imagined Tim had wrapped the women in. Samuel allowed himself a grim smile. They were getting careless, confident in their escape. A rookie mistake he'd seen countless defendants make.

Ahead, the ground showed signs of rest – compressed grass where bodies had lain, distinctive boot prints in a patch of mud. Fresh. Large. Buck's size. Samuel traced the signs with his eyes, noting where the undergrowth had been recently disturbed. They couldn't be more than an hour ahead.

Samuel checked his map again, though the movement sent fresh pain through his shoulder. The road couldn't be more than two miles away. If they were stopping to rest, this might be his best chance. But what could one injured man do against two experienced killers?

The lawyer in him wanted to wait, to plan, to calculate odds. His knee screamed for rest, the swelling already visible. But Monica's voice whispered again: "Sometimes the heart knows better than the head."

Samuel tucked the map away and began moving forward, staying low, staying quiet. A vulture landed in a dead tree ahead, as if expecting the violence to come. He had no weapon, no working phone, no backup plan. But he had something Buck and Tim weren't counting on... he had absolutely nothing left to lose.

CHAPTER 20

SHADOWS OF SALVATION

Samuel's knee gave out without warning, sending him crashing to the ground. Sharp rocks bit into his palms as he tried to break his fall. The pain was immediate and intense – something had torn, something important.

"No, no, no," he groaned, trying to stand. His knee buckled again, refusing to bear weight. He crawled to a fallen log, the movement jarring his already broken ribs. The afternoon sun beat down mercilessly as he slumped against the rough bark.

"I can't," he whispered to no one. "I can't do this."

His mind began to drift, exhaustion and pain blurring the edges of reality. What was he really trying to prove here? That he could save Collette and Shannon when he could not even save his own wife?

Monica's face floated before him – not from their happy beach photo, but from that last morning. The way she'd looked at him across the breakfast table, dark circles under her eyes from another sleepless night. "I can't do another round," she'd said. "I can't keep putting my body through this while you're too busy with cases to even make it to the appointments."

"We'll try again when the Jensen merger is done," Samuel promised, not even looking up from his briefing documents. "Just give it time."

Time. He'd always thought they had more time.

The sun seemed to pulse overhead, each beat driving him further into the past. That final voicemail he had never returned. The unopened bottle of prenatal vitamins in their bathroom cabinet. The way her mother had looked at him at the funeral, silent accusation in her eyes.

Samuel's head lolled back against the log. He was so tired. So damn tired.

The world began to fade, and suddenly he was in the water again. The current pulled at him, trying to drag him under. His head barely stayed above the surface as waves crashed over him. Through the turbulent water, he saw her – the woman in the purple dress, standing impossibly still against the chaos.

This time she turned, looking back over her shoulder. Samuel caught a glimpse of her profile through the spray, her face almost visible—

A car door slammed.

Samuel jerked awake, disoriented. How long had he been out? The sun had shifted, casting longer shadows. His body felt leaden, unresponsive.

"Oh my God, Samuel?" Ranger Florence's voice cut through his fog. She hurried toward him, her red hair catching the late afternoon light. "What happened to you?"

"Buck," Samuel managed, his throat raw. "Tim. They... they killed Daniel. Took Collette and Shannon. Trafficking." The words tumbled out in a desperate rush.

"Slow down," Florence knelt beside him, her face a mask of concern. "Oh boy You're dehydrated and injured. Let's get you to my station. I'll radio for help."

She reached for her radio, speaking clearly: "This is Ranger Florence. I need medical aid and law enforcement at Station 7. Possible assault victims, two missing hikers." She paused, listening to static. "Copy that. Will transport survivors to station and await backup."

Relief flooded through Samuel. Finally, help came. They could still save Collette and Shannon.

"Can you walk?" Florence asked, helping him up. "My vehicle's just up on the service road."

Samuel's knee screamed in protest as she supported him, but the promise of rescue gave him strength. He hobbled alongside her, each step an agony.

"Tell me everything," she urged as they moved. "About Buck and Tim."

Samuel explained in broken sentences – the shooting, the syringes, his fall, the logging road rendezvous. Florence nodded sympathetically, guiding him toward a park service SUV.

"You've been through quite an ordeal," she said, helping him into the passenger seat. "We'll get this sorted out at the station. Help is on the way."

Samuel's head fell back against the headrest as Florence started the engine. His whole body felt heavy, his thoughts moving like molasses. Something nagged at the edge of his consciousness – something about the radio call, about Florence's reaction to Buck and Tim's names.

But he was so tired. So very tired.

"Rest now," Florence's voice seemed to come from far away. "Everything will be clear soon."

As the SUV rolled through the growing shadows, Samuel's eyes drifted closed. He thought he heard Florence making another call, but he could not be certain.

His last coherent thought was of the woman in his dream, turning to show her face. Had it been Monica? Or had it been something else – a warning he hadn't heeded?

The SUV carried him deeper into the gathering dusk, toward a rescue that was anything but, while somewhere in the canyon, two women's lives hung in the balance, and a dark enterprise continued its brutal work.

CHAPTER 21

WHEN HELP HURTS

Samuel's eyes fluttered open to the sterile glare of fluorescent lights. He was lying on an examination table, his wounds cleaned and bandaged. The sharp antiseptic smell reminded him of hospitals, of sitting beside Monica during failed procedures.

"Hello?" His voice cracked.

A small desk with a computer occupied one corner of the station, its screen displaying standard park service screensavers. First aid supplies lined metal shelves, meticulously organized. Everything looked official, proper – too proper, like a movie set version of a ranger station.

A plate of bread and a large glass of orange juice sat on a small table beside him. Samuel's parched throat ached at the sight. He grabbed the juice, taking several deep swallows before his lawyer's instincts kicked in. When did Florence had time to prepare this?

Testing his injured knee, Samuel eased himself off the table. Pain shot through his leg, but it held. He limped to the window, taking in his surroundings. Station 7 sat in a small clearing, surrounded by dense forest. A shed-like structure stood about fifty feet away with a heavy

padlock gleaming on its door. Something about it seemed wrong –
the reinforced hinges, the deadbolt, the small ventilation slots near the
roof.

Another door inside the station caught his attention – solid wood
with a heavy deadbolt. Not standard park service issue. Samuel's pulse
quickened as his mind cataloged these inconsistencies like evidence in
a case.

"Hello?" he called again, louder this time. "Ranger Florence?
Where's the police?"

Rapid footsteps approached, and Florence burst into the room.
She'd changed out of her ranger uniform into jeans and a black T-shirt,
her red hair pulled back severely from her face. The transformation
was subtle but significant – like an actor stepping out of costume.

"You shouldn't be up," she said firmly, guiding him back to the
examination table. "You need rest. Finish your juice."

"The police—"

"Shh...quiet, rest. Do not worry they are on their way," she cut him
off, pushing the juice glass toward him. "Drink. You're dehydrated."

Samuel lifted the glass to his lips, pretending to sip. A metallic taste
lingered on his tongue from his earlier drinks. Lead? No – something
else. Something pharmaceutical.

"You've been through quite an ordeal," Florence continued, watching him intently. "The juice will help with your injuries it's full of
vitamins."

Samuel let his eyelids droop, his movements becoming sluggish.
"You're right," he slurred slightly. "So tired."

Florence's face softened with satisfaction. "Sleep," she urged.
"Everything will be taken care of soon."

Samuel's legal mind raced behind his facade of drowsiness. The
locked door. The reinforced shed. The drugged juice. The missing

backup. Like pieces of a case falling into place, revealing a picture he should have seen sooner.

"Just need to..." he mumbled, letting his eyes close. His breathing deepened, body going limp.

Florence watched him for several long moments. Samuel forced himself to remain still, fighting every instinct to flinch when she checked his pulse. Finally satisfied, she moved away.

The walkie-talkie crackled to life. Florence stepped into the hallway, but Samuel could still hear her clearly.

"T here. Package is secured. Primary assets en route to delivery point. Secondary package prepped for cleanup. Over."

A male voice responded – Buck's. "Copy that, Mother. Tim's got the girls prepped. Buyers waiting at the airstrip. Transport will come to the meeting point to take the assets. ETA three hours. Over."

"Understood. I'll meet you there after disposal. Out."

Mother. The word hit Samuel like another bullet. Florence was their mother. T. The mastermind.

He heard her gathering things in the other room, moving with purpose. The keys jingled, then the main door opened and closed. A lock turned.

Samuel waited, counting his breaths. The click of a car door, an engine starting, gravel crunching as the vehicle pulled away. Still, he waited, making sure it wasn't a test.

Finally, he opened his eyes. His head swam – whatever she had put in the juice was strong, but his limited consumption and size had worked in his favor. He needed to move fast, before the drugs took full effect.

The station felt different now, its ordinary surfaces concealing darker purposes. That locked room – how many others had been held there? The shed outside – a temporary holding cell? How long had this family been using Canyon Park as their hunting ground?

Samuel hobbled to the window again. Florence's vehicle was gone. The sun was setting, painting the clearing in blood-red light. Three hours until the buyers met at the airstrip. Three hours before Collette and Shannon disappeared forever.

Samuel asked himself, could he find a way out. Could he fight through the drugs in his system. Could his body take more punishment.

The taste of drugged juice lingered in his mouth like an accusation. He did not save Monica. Did not stop Buck at Eagle's Point. Did not see through Florence's rescue ruse.

But, just maybe, he had not failed completely. Not yet.

Samuel turned from the window, scanning the room with a new purpose. Florence had cleaned his wounds, restored some of his strength. Now he just had to figure out how to use her own station against her.

Somewhere in these mountains, a family of monsters prepared to sell two innocent women. They thought Samuel was safely held, ready for "disposal."

They were about to learn how dangerous a desperate man could be.

Time to tear their operation apart, piece by piece.

CHAPTER 22

Three-Way Dance of Desperation

Tim's legs trembled with exhaustion. They had been carrying the women for hours, and Shannon's dead weight seemed to grow heavier with each step. Tim's foot caught on a root, and he stumbled, losing his grip. Shannon rolled from his shoulders, hitting the ground with a dull thud.

A soft moan escaped her lips.

"Shit!" Buck set Collette down roughly, storming over to his brother. "You fucking idiot! What did I tell you about damaging the merchandise?"

Tim scrambled to check Shannon's pulse. "I'm sorry, I'm sorry! She's starting to wake up. I need to give her another dose—"

"Then do it!" Buck towered over him; fists clenched.

Unknown to both men, Collette lay perfectly still, her mind racing beneath closed eyelids. The drugs had worn off a few miles back on their trek, but she had forced herself to stay limp, waiting. Waiting for a moment just like this.

Tim frantically dug through his backpack, empty syringes clattering. His face went pale. "They're... they're gone. I must have dropped the last ones when we crossed the ridge."

Buck grabbed Tim by the throat. "You worthless piece of—"

The rock connected with the back of Buck's head with a sickening crack. He stumbled forward, releasing Tim, who fell backward in shock. Collette stood behind them, her bound hands still raised, a bloody stone clutched between them.

"Shannon!" Collette screamed, trying to reach her friend. But Shannon only moaned softly, still deep under sedation.

Making a split-second decision, Collette turned and bolted into the forest. Her cross-training kicked in as she leaped over fallen logs and ducked under branches, her tied hands held tight against her chest.

"Get her!" Buck roared, blood trickling down his neck. "Don't let her reach the main trail!"

Tim scrambled to his feet, crashing through the undergrowth after Collette. But she was faster, more agile, her regular running routine paying off as she widened the gap between them. Tim's desperate footfalls grew fainter behind her.

Buck grabbed his radio, cursing. "T! We have a situation. One asset is lost in sector four. Moving east toward the ridge line. Tim's in pursuit but he's useless as always."

Back at Station 7, Samuel's head snapped up at the sound of Buck's voice. A spare radio crackled to life on the desk, forgotten in Florence's haste to leave.

"Copy that," Florence's voice replied. "Don't let her reach the park boundaries. Take her down if you must. We can't risk exposure."

***

Samuel forced himself up, fighting through the drug's effects. The radio was his link to the outside, his chance to call for real help. But it sat on the desk beyond the locked door.

He examined the lock, his legal training suddenly useful in an unexpected way. How many times had he cross-examined locksmiths and questioned security experts? He knew how these mechanisms worked, at least in theory.

"Asset continuing east," Buck's voice crackled again on the radio. "Tim's lost visual contact. I'm securing the other package and moving to higher ground for sight lines."

Samuel looked around frantically, spotting a wire coat hanger on a rack. He grabbed it with trembling hands, straightening the wire while mentally reciting testimony from an old case about lock picking.

***

Collette ran, her cross-training instincts taking over. Each step precise despite her bound hands, each breath measured like she was running hill sprints back home. But this was not her morning workout route – this was survival.

The forest blurred past as branches whipped her face. She could hear Tim crashing through the undergrowth behind her, his movements clumsy compared to her athletic precision. Her mind flashed to Daniel's body crumpling. Samuel, tumbling into space. All while she had been busy flirting with their murderer.

She found cover behind a massive boulder, her lungs burning. God, she had been so stupid. The midnight swim, the coy glances at Buck.

Samuel had tried to warn them. Samuel had seen the predator while she'd been admiring its teeth.

"Please!" Tim's voice carried through the trees. "Stop! They'll kill me if you escape!"

Collette pressed herself against the cool stone, memories flooding back. The way Buck had looked at her in the river, not like a woman but like prey. How had she mistaken that hunger for attraction? And Shannon – drugged, helpless, she's counting on her. The thought of her friend's life in her hands made her stomach turn.

She had to make a choice. Run for help, leaving Shannon behind? Or try something desperate? Her hand found a rock, smooth and heavy. A weapon.

Footsteps approached. Collette tightened her grip on the stone.

"I see you," Tim's voice trembled closer. "Please. You don't understand what they'll do—"

"What you'll do, you mean," Collette stepped out. "Your part of this."

"You don't understand anything," Tim's face twisted with hurt. "I saw you; you know. In the river with him. After our talk, after you pretended to care—"

"Tim—"

"Just like Eve. Women always choose him." His laugh was bitter. "Even when we were gathering wood, you were thinking about him, weren't you? Poor, weak Tim. Good for a sympathetic ear while you plot to get his brother's attention."

"That's not—"

"Save it!" Tim's voice cracked. "I thought... when you helped me with the firewood, talked to me about love... but you're all the same. Using me to get to him."

Collette's mind raced. The cliff edge was close – she could hear the river below. She needed to keep him talking.

"I was wrong about Buck," she said carefully. "We all were. Help me, Tim. Help Shannon. You're better than this—"

"Better?" Tim's laugh was edged with hysteria. "There is no better. There's just survival. Buck showed me that. Over and over."

"Then why help me up when I stumbled on the trail?" Collette took a step back, feeling loose rocks shift under her feet. "There's still good in you, Tim."

For a moment, something flickered in Tim's eyes – doubt, maybe hope. But then his radio crackled.

On the cliff edge, Collette held Tim's gaze, her bound hands raised defensively. The setting sun painted the canyon in shades of amber and shadow, like nature's spotlight on their final act.

"Tim, please," she said softly. "Remember what we talked about, when we were getting firewood? I wasn't being honest with you."

He took a step forward, something clutched behind his back. "Don't. Don't try to manipulate me."

"I have been in love," Collette continued, her voice breaking. "With Samuel, in college. But I was scared – scared of being vulnerable, of letting someone see the real me. So, I ran." Tears streaked down her dirt-stained face. "I pushed him toward Monica because it was easier than facing my own fears. Then I spent years being jealous of what they had, bitter about what I'd thrown away."

Tim's hand tightened around something behind his back. "Stop talking."

"You were right about love, Tim. About regret. I shouldn't have been angry at Samuel – I should have been angry at myself. But that doesn't mean it's too late." She took a careful step forward. "You've been loved before. You can be loved again. Just like I can. Just give me that chance."

Tim's face contorted. "I saw you, with Buck. In the river. You are just like Eve – just like all of them. Using people, playing games."

"No, Tim, that's not—"

Collette sprung forward, thinking she could overpower him. She saw the surprise in his eyes and felt a moment of triumph – then the sharp sting in her neck.

"I saved one," Tim whispered as she stumbled as he plunged the syringe in her neck.

The world began to tilt sideways as the ketamine flooded her system. The last thing she saw was Tim's sad face as he keyed his radio.

"Asset secured," he reported tonelessly. "Location Widow's Peak."

As consciousness faded, Collette's last thought was of Shannon. Of Samuel, trying to warn them. Of all the warnings she should have heeded, all the signs she should have seen.

***

At Station 7, Samuel worked the straightened wire into the lock, feeling for the mechanisms he had heard described in court. His hands shook from the drugs and sweat dripped into his eyes.

The radio squawked again. "All units, asset last seen entering ravine system near marker 22. Converge and contain."

Samuel's makeshift lock pick suddenly caught on something. He held his breath, applying gentle pressure the way that expert witness had described years ago. The lock clicked.

"Package two secure," Buck radioed. "Moving to intercept point beta. Tim, report position."

Static answered.

"Tim, report position NOW!"

More static.

Samuel eased the door open, his heart pounding. The radio sat on the desk, tantalizingly close. If he could just figure out how to change channels, reach actual park services...

The radio at Station 7 crackled one final time: "Asset cornered at Widow's Peak. Moving to retrieve."

Samuel grabbed the radio, his fingers dancing across the controls. Somewhere in these mountains, Collette was fighting for her life. He had to find the right frequency; he had to get word out.

Time was running out for all of them.

Samuel frantically turned the radio dial, but each channel yielded only static or silence. Something wasn't right – park service radios were needed to keep clear channels for emergencies. He examined the device closer, noting its custom modifications. This wasn't standard park equipment at all.

Frustrated, he turned to the laptop on the desk. Password protected, of course. Samuel's mind raced, remembering countless cybersecurity depositions. People often chose passwords connected to their identities, their secrets.

His eyes swept the room, landing on a faded poster behind the desk – Mr. T from the A-Team, wearing his signature gold chains. The radio call sign "T," the way Buck had said "Mother"...

Samuel's fingers moved across the keyboard: MommaT

The screen unlocked.

A chat window was already open, the interface sleek and encrypted. "Heaven's Gifts International Import/Export" headed the conversation. Samuel's stomach turned as he read:

HG_Coordinator: Assets confirmed? Quality verification needed before wire transfer.

T_Handler: Two females. Ages 28 and 32. Physically fit, no marks. Blonde American, brunette American. Photos attached.

HG_Coordinator: Perfect demographic for São Paulo client. $100K USD each. Usual terms.

T_Handler: Transport arranged via private charter. McCarran International, terminal 3. ETA 2300 hours.

HG_Coordinator: Zurich account ready for deposit. Client expects undamaged merchandise.

Samuel scrolled through the chat history, his lawyer's mind cataloging evidence. Heaven's Gifts was a front, their professional terminology masking brutal human trafficking. They operated globally, with contacts in Brazil, Eastern Europe, and Southeast Asia.

A spreadsheet caught his eye: "Inventory_2018-2024.xlsx"

Opening it revealed Florence's meticulous records. Thirty-four women over six years, each categorized by physical attributes, sale price, and destination. Notes in the margins referenced "collection points" throughout Canyon Park.

The pieces clicked together. Florence's ranger position gave her perfect cover – access to remote areas, authority to close trails, ability to explain away disappearances as hiking accidents. The park was her hunting ground, and she'd been using it for years.

Samuel pulled up a web browser, hands shaking as he typed in the Sacramento Police Department's website. He found their tip line chat feature and quickly typed:

"Human trafficking operation at Canyon Park. Station 7. Ranger Florence involved. Two victims are in immediate danger. Multiple suspects. Evidence on laptop at station."

The message was not sent. An instant automatic reply came up on the screen, "mailbox not monitored".

"Dammit!" Samuel slammed his fist on the desk. His eyes darted around the room – there had to be another way to call for help.

Lost and found. Every ranger station had one.

He spotted a locked drawer under the desk. The wire hanger was already bent from the door lock, but it would have to do. This lock was simpler, designed more to prevent casual snooping than determined entry.

The drawer popped open after thirty seconds of manipulation. Inside lay a collection of items: sunglasses, car keys, water bottles, a pocketknife, and – thank God – a smartphone with its charger.

Samuel grabbed the phone and charger, plugging it into the wall outlet. The screen remained dark.

"Come on, come on," he muttered, holding the power button. After what felt like an eternity, the Apple logo appeared.

No SIM card, but it still had its emergency call capability. As soon as it booted up, Samuel dialed 911.

"911, what's your emergency?"

"Listen carefully," Samuel spoke rapidly. "I'm at Canyon Park Station 7. There is an active human trafficking operation. Two women have been kidnapped. The kidnappers are armed and—"

The line went dead.

Samuel looked up to see the phone charger's cord severed, and Florence standing in the doorway with a hunting knife.

"Lawyers," she said, her ranger facade completely gone. "Always so thorough with your evidence gathering." She gestured at the laptop with her knife. "Finding anything interesting in my files?"

Samuel's mind raced. Had the call gone through? Had they traced it? Would help come?

"Did you really think I'd leave an operational phone where prisoners could find it?" Florence stepped into the room, closing the door behind her. "That was a test, Samuel. One you just failed."

She raised the radio to her lips. "Buck, status report."

"Package two secured," Buck's voice crackled. "Asset one cornered. Moving to cleanup phase."

Florence smiled coldly. "Excellent. I'll handle cleanup here as well."

Samuel gripped the pocketknife from the drawer behind his back, knowing he was out of options. He'd found the evidence, made the call. Now he just had to stay alive long enough for help to arrive.

If help was coming at all.

The sun had almost set outside, casting the room in blood-red light. Somewhere in these mountains, Collette was fighting for her life. Shannon was being "secured" for transport. And here in Station 7, Samuel faced a woman who had spent years sending others to their deaths.

His fingers tightened on the pocketknife as Florence approached. He might not be able to save everyone.

But he could make damn sure this station claimed its last victim today.

***

Inside Station 7, Florence turned toward her radio, reaching to respond. That moment of distraction was all Samuel needed.

He launched himself forward, pocketknife aimed at her kidney. But Florence was faster than she looked. She pivoted, driving her knee directly into his injured one.

Samuel's scream echoed off the station walls as white-hot agony exploded through his leg. He crumpled, the knife clattering from his grip. Florence's boot crashed down on his groin, driving whatever breath remained from his lungs.

"Men," she sneered, delivering a savage kick to his head. "Always thinking with the wrong head."

Darkness claimed him before he hit the floor.

Tim gathered Collette's unconscious form, her earlier words echoing in his head. Love. Chance. Regret. He pushed the thoughts away as he began the trek back to where Buck waited with Shannon.

"Did she cry?" Buck called out as Tim approached. "They always cry at the end."

Tim said nothing, carefully laying Collette next to Shannon's still form.

"Help me get them up," Buck commanded. "Mom wants them cleaned up before the buyers see them. Can't have them looking like they've been dragged through the woods." He laughed at his own joke.

As they hoisted the women onto their shoulders one final time, Tim allowed himself one last look at Collette's face. For a moment, he saw all the Collette's they had taken over the years. All the women who had begged for chances they'd never get.

Back at Station 7, Florence surveyed Samuel's crumpled form with cold efficiency. The failed rescue attempt would add flavor to the official story – grieving widower, driven mad by loss, taking unnecessary risks in the wilderness. They would find his body at the bottom of a cliff, another tragic accident in a park that had seen so many.

She keyed her radio: "Station 7 secured. Cleanup in progress. Proceed with delivery."

The sun finally set, darkness claiming the canyon. Somewhere in the gathering night, two unconscious women were being carried toward their fate. In a ranger station that had become a processing center for human cargo, a battered man lay bleeding on the floor.

And in the space between rescue and damnation, the river continued its eternal flow, carrying secrets deeper into the canyon's unforgiving heart.

The night was far from over. And Station 7 had not claimed its last victim.

CHAPTER 23

EARTH'S DARK BAPTISM

The water pressed in from all sides, dark and cold, filling Samuel's lungs. He thrashed against the current, legs kicking uselessly as he sank deeper. Through the murky depths, a figure appeared above the surface – just a shadow against the fading light. A hand plunged into the water, reaching for him...

A car door slam jolted Samuel back to consciousness. His head throbbed; dried blood crusted around his eyes. Cold wood pressed against his cheek, and his hands burned from the zip ties cutting into his wrists. He must be in the shed. Florence's "cleanup" location.

Pushing himself to his knees, Samuel crawled to the wall, using it to steady himself as he peered through a gap in the wooden slats. Florence's truck sat in the growing darkness, its headlights illuminating Buck and Tim as they carefully lifted two limp forms from the back seat.

Collette and Shannon, still unconscious, their bodies hanging like broken dolls in the brothers' arms.

"Get them inside," Florence's voice carried across the yard. "We need to clean them up before transport. And handle our other problems." She glanced toward the shed.

Samuel's heart hammered against his ribs as they disappeared into Station 7. He had minutes, less, before they came for him.

Focus. Think. Analyze the situation like a case.

His legal mind kicked in, cataloging resources and options. The shed's interior came into sharp focus as his eyes adjusted to the dim light. Tools hung on the wall – remnants of actual ranger maintenance work, or implements for darker purposes? A nail gun dangled from a hook; its power cord coiled beneath it. Next to it, a flathead screwdriver showed signs of frequent use, its handle worn smooth.

More importantly, the floorboards beneath him felt loose, one corner slightly raised. Samuel shifted his weight, hearing the wood creak. If he could pry it up...

But first, the zip ties.

He had cross-examined a security expert once about restraint devices. Zip ties had a locking mechanism – a small tab that caught the ridges. If you could insert something thin enough between the tab and the ridges...

Samuel maneuvered himself to his feet, turning his back to the screwdriver. His fingers, numb from the restraints, fumbled as he tried to grasp the tool. The first attempt sent it clattering to the floor.

"Shit," he hissed, dropping back down. He could hear voices from Station 7, the sound of water running. They were cleaning up their "merchandise."

Second attempt. His fingers closed around the screwdriver's handle. Twisting his wrists at an agonizing angle, he worked the flat edge between the zip tie's ridges and tab. The plastic fought him, digging deeper into his flesh.

Push steady pressure. Don't rush. Don't—

The zip tie snapped.

Samuel bit back a groan as blood rushed back into his hands. No time to celebrate. He dropped to his knees, examining the loose floorboard. The nails had rusted, their heads protruding slightly.

Perfect.

Using the screwdriver as a lever, he worked it under the board's edge. Wood creaked as he applied pressure. One nail popped free, then another. He froze at each sound, expecting the door to burst open, expecting Florence's cold smile to be his last sight.

But the voices in Station 7 continued, preoccupied with their grim work.

The board came free with a subtle groan, revealing packed earth beneath. Samuel examined the gap – maybe eighteen inches of clearance. Tight, but manageable. The foundation's edge would be just past the shed's wall.

He grabbed the nail gun, checking its weight. Still loaded. The screwdriver went into his back pocket.

He heard new sounds from Station 7 – drawers opening, metal clinking. They were almost done with their preparations.

Samuel lowered himself into the gap, dragging the board partially back into place behind him. The earth pressed against his chest as he wormed forward, trying to control his breathing. Each inch felt like a mile, the packed dirt scraping his face, filling his nose with the smell of decay.

How many others had died in this shed? How many bodies had this earth absorbed?

Light appeared ahead – the gap between foundation and ground. Samuel appeared like a creature birthing itself from the earth, covered in dirt, blood, and desperation.

Keeping low, he crept toward Station 7. Through a window, he could see Florence preparing syringes while Buck and Tim dressed the unconscious women in clean clothes. Getting them ready for "delivery."

The nail gun felt heavy in Samuel's grip as he watched them work. He had no real plan, no backup, no guarantee he could save anyone. But he had surprise on his side, and the kind of fury that only comes from having nothing left to lose.

Above him, the first stars appeared in the darkening sky. Somewhere in the distance, the river's endless rush reminded him of his dream – of that hand reaching down through the water.

It had not been trying to save him after all.

It had been showing him what he needed to become.

CHAPTER 24

THIS TIME HE FIGHTS

S amuel pressed against the window, watching Florence preparing to inject something into Collette's arm. His attention caught on Shannon's hand – subtle movement, a finger twitch. She was conscious, fighting through the drugs, but keeping her eyes closed.

He needed her to see him. To know help was coming. But any obvious signal would alert their captors.

A fist-sized rock lay by the foundation. Samuel grabbed it, calculating trajectory like a physics problem. The rock arced through the darkness, landing on the station's metal roof with a sharp crack.

"The hell was that?" Buck straightened.

"Check outside," Florence snapped, moving toward the door.

Samuel flattened himself against the wall as all three stepped onto the porch, boots crunching on gravel. The moment they cleared the room, he tapped the window softly.

"Shannon," he whispered. "Collette."

Shannon's eyes fluttered open. Recognition flickered across her face before she quickly resumed her feigned unconsciousness.

"Probably raccoons," Tim's voice carried from outside.

Florence strode back in first. "Check the perimeter. Both of you. All of it."

Florence set down her syringe, her ranger persona dropping away like a shed skin. She moved to the women with predatory grace, running the back of her hand over Collette's exposed neck. "

Samuel flattened himself against the wall as Buck and Tim stepped outside. Through the window, he watched Florence trace her fingers along Collette's jawline. "This one might fetch a bonus," she purred. "Perfect bone structure."

Tim shuffled back in first. "Buck already had a taste. At the river last night."

Florence's hand froze. Her face contorted with rage. "What did you say?"

Buck swaggered in, grinning. "Didn't leave a mark, Mom. Just having some fun—"

The crack of Florence's hand across Buck's face echoed through the station. "You stupid animal! How many times have you damaged the merchandise? She struck him again. "Your little dick is going to ruin everything!"

Buck, face reddening with humiliation, pointed at Tim. "Well Tim wanted to quit on the mountain today! Said he was done with all this—"

"Because he respects the business!" Florence grabbed Buck's ear like he was a child. "Your brother knows better than to damage my merchandise." Her voice dropped to a venomous whisper. "I had nothing when your worthless father left us for that pretty little stripper. Nothing! But look at me now."

She gestured at the unconscious women. "They're all the same. Pretty young things who think the world owes them everything. They took my husband, my life – now I take them. I built this operation from nothing while you two played soldier and boy scout."

Florence shoved Buck toward the door. "Go check the shed. Make sure our friend is still sleeping. And keep your hands to yourself – that's all you're good for anyway."

"Tim, stay with me." Her voice softened. "I know you won't mess with Mama's merchandise."

Samuel was already crawling back to the shed, bile rising in his throat. He dove through the gap in the floorboards, plugging in the nail gun with trembling hands to the outlet on the shed wall. The cord snaked across the floor as he positioned himself, playing dead.

***

Buck's boots approached. Metal scraped against metal as he worked the padlock. The door creaked open.

Buck's massive frame filled the shed's doorway. "Rise and shine, Lincoln," he sneered, closing the door behind him. The nail gun felt slick in Samuel's sweating hands as he played dead, waiting.

A boot connected with his ribs. "I said wake up!"

Samuel rolled, bringing the nail gun up, but Buck was faster than his size suggested. His hand clamped around Samuel's wrist, forcing the weapon aside as the first shot went wide.

"There he is!" Buck laughed, applying crushing pressure. "The big brave Lincoln lawyer! Come on, show me what they teach you in law school."

They grappled in the cramped space, Buck's superior strength forcing Samuel back. The nail gun wavered between them.

"You couldn't protect your wife," Buck taunted through gritted teeth. "Couldn't save that pretty boy Daniel. What makes you think—"

The mention of Monica ignited something in Samuel's chest. Not the careful, controlled rage of cross-examination, but something primal. His elbow shot up, catching Buck's throat. The larger man's grip loosened just enough.

The nail gun barked. The first shot caught Buck's left eye, the impact throwing his head back. His scream of shock and rage filled the shed as Samuel fired again, the second nail punching through his gaping mouth.

But Buck didn't fall. Blood spraying, he lunged forward, his remaining eyes wide with disbelief. His hands found Samuel's throat. "You... fucking..."

Samuel squeezed the trigger again. Again. Neck. Chest. Face. Each impact jerked Buck's massive body, but still he came, driven by the same brutality that had defined his life.

"Can't... stop... me..." Buck growled through the blood, nails protruding from his face like metal whiskers.

In that moment, Samuel saw himself in Buck's remaining eye – the coldness, the calculation, the disregard for others' pain. Everything that had driven Monica into that bathtub.

Something broke loose inside him. Every suppressed emotion, every moment of helplessness, every failure to save someone he loved – it all poured out through his finger on the trigger. His roar matched Buck's animal fury as he emptied the nail gun into his attacker's body.

"This is for Monica!" Another nail. "For Daniel!" Two more. "For every woman you've hurt!"

The nails created a grotesque constellation across Buck's flesh until finally, finally, he collapsed. His face was a metal sculpture, his last expression frozen in shocked recognition that his victim had become the predator.

Samuel caught his reflection in a shard of broken glass – blood-streaked, dirt-caked, eyes burning with something between madness and justice. He barely recognized himself. The careful, controlled lawyer was gone. Something new had been forged in violence and vengeance.

Focus Samuel. Buck had a gun. He slowly reached his hand to Bucks back, no gun. Buck's gun had to be here.

It must be in the jeep. Samuel crawled out his escape route one final time. He slowly moved to the jeep. The gun lay under the seat, a silencer attached. Three bullets in the magazine.

Through the station window, Florence prepared another syringe while Tim hovered nearby. Samuel checked his reflection in the truck's window – blood-streaked, dirt-caked, eyes burning with something between madness and justice.

Three bullets. Two monsters. One chance to end it all.

He had crawled out from under the shed like being born again, emerging from an earthen womb into the harsh light. The man who had calculated odds and watched his wife drown in grief had died in that shed alongside Buck. What emerged was something else – something forged in blood and justified rage.

The lawyer was dead. The warrior had risen.

***

Samuel crept toward the station's rear, gun steady despite his injuries. Through the window, he saw Florence who was no longer concealing the monster beneath. The station's fluorescent lights cast sickly shadows across medical supplies and restraints – tools of her true profession.

Through the drug-induced haze, Collette's consciousness flickered. The sharp medicinal smell, the cold metal table beneath her, Florence's humming as she prepared the assets – each sensation pierced the fog like distant lightning.

Shannon exploded into action first, launching herself upward with fingers curled like claws. Blood welled from the deep scratches across Tim's face as he screamed, stumbling backward.

"You little bitch!" Florence dropped the syringe, rushing to restrain Shannon.

In that moment, Collette – running on pure instinct – sprang up and leaped onto Florence's back. Her unbound hands locked around the older woman's throat as they stumbled across the room, knocking over a tray of medical supplies that clattered like broken wind chimes.

Florence slammed Collette against the wall. "I'll kill you both myself!"

Tim recovered enough to grab Shannon, driving his knee into her back. The scene dissolved into chaos – screaming, fighting, bodies colliding in the cramped space.

Samuel had no choice. He sprinted to the front door, driving his shoulder into it. The wood splintered as he burst in, firing wildly as he ran. The first shot went wide, punching a hole in the wall.

Florence spun toward him, her face transforming from rage to cruel amusement. "Well, look who came back to play hero. Didn't get enough of a fall the first time?"

"Buck won't be joining us," Samuel said coldly. "He's taking a permanent nap in the shed."

Florence's eyes widened, but not with maternal grief. "You fool!" she snarled, reaching behind her back. "Do you know what those buyers are paying? What you have cost me?" Her ranger facade cracked completely, revealing decades of bitterness beneath. "These pretty little things think they deserve everything – now they'll learn what it means to have nothing!"

Collette's vision cleared enough to see Samuel standing in the doorway, gun aimed at Florence's heart. Blood and dirt caked his clothes, but his hands were steady. Through swollen eyes, she saw the lawyer she'd known transformed into something else – something forged in violence and justice.

"The only thing they'll learn," Samuel said, "is that you picked the wrong prey."

Florence lunged with surprising speed, a hidden blade glinting in her hand. But Samuel's finger was already squeezing the trigger. The shot caught her in the stomach, the impact spinning her around. Blood blossomed across her black shirt as she crumpled, howling in pain and rage.

"Shit!" she shrieked, trying to staunch the blood. "You're ruining everything!"

Collette pounced at once, her hands finding Florence's throat again. "You like selling women?" she snarled, fingers tightening. "How does it feel to be powerless?"

"Mom!" Tim released Shannon, starting forward. "No!"

Samuel's gun swung toward him. "One bullet left, Tim. Your choice."

"Shoot him!" Collette yelled, still choking Florence, whose struggles were weakening. "End this!"

"Where's the meetup point?" Samuel demanded Tim. "The buyers – where are they coming?"

"I don't... I can't..."

"Bullshit!" Samuel's finger tightened on the trigger. "Your brother's dead, your mother's dying. You are alone. Where is the meetup?"

Tim broke. "Old mining road, three miles east. Abandoned quarry. They're coming at 10."

"Down. On your knees. Samuel commanded. "Shannon watch his back."

Shannon, rubbing her bruised back, got up and diligently watched Tim. Her hands shook as she glared at Tim.

"Give me the radio," Samuel commanded as he put it in Tim's face. "Tell them plans changed. Tell them to come to Station 7 instead."

Tim looked at his mother, still gasping under Collette's grip. "I... I can't..."

Samuel pressed the gun against his temple. "Do it."

Tim's voice trembled as he keyed the radio: "Base, this is pickup team. Change of location. Assets will be at Station 7. Repeat, proceed to Station 7 for collection."

The radio crackled: "Copy that. ETA forty minutes."

Florence's struggles had ceased, her eyes glassy. Collette released her throat, scrambling backward. "Is she...?"

"No, shes Unconscious," Samuel confirmed, checking Florence's pulse. "But alive. Unfortunately."

Collette stood on shaky legs and threw herself into Samuel's arms. "I was wrong about you," she whispered. "So wrong. You came back for us."

"Always," he murmured into her hair, allowing himself one moment of relief before turning to Shannon. "You, okay?"

Shannon nodded, though tears streaked her face. "What... what do we do now?"

Samuel checked his watch. Forty minutes until the buyers arrived. Forty minutes to set a trap for an international trafficking ring. His lawyer's mind was already building the case, cataloging evidence.

"First, we secure these two properly. Then we call in every law enforcement agency within range." He looked at Tim, huddled on the floor. "Your mother's operation ends tonight."

"You don't understand," Tim whimpered. "You don't know how far this goes, who's involved..."

"I saw the files, Tim. All of them. Every woman you helped sell. Every life you helped destroy." Samuel's voice was ice. "It's over."

Collette went to Shannon, holding her as they both shook with delayed shock and relief. The adrenaline was wearing off, reality setting in.

Samuel kept his gun trained on Tim while checking Florence's pulse. His body ached, his injuries screaming for attention. But there would be time for pain later. Time for processing all of this later.

Right now, they had forty minutes to prepare for the next phase. Forty minutes before more monsters arrived, expecting to find merchandise but finding justice instead.

The river's roar had faded to a whisper, as if nature itself was holding its breath. In the distance, thunder rolled – a storm approaching, or just the sound of retribution drawing near.

Samuel looked at the women he had saved, at the evil he had stopped. For the first time since Monica's death, he felt something like peace.

The case wasn't closed yet. But the verdict was already in.

CHAPTER 25

Dawn's Red Redemption

"We need a plan," Samuel muttered, searching Buck's backpack. His fingers closed around his phone – still charged. "Evidence first."

He quickly recorded the scene: Florence dying on the station floor and Tim on his knees frozen as Shannon held the gun to him, the medical supplies, the laptop with its damning files. Collette began rummaging through drawers, collecting potential weapons.

"Here," she called, holding up a taser and pepper spray. "Standard ranger equipment."

Headlights suddenly swept across the windows.

"Tim!" Samuel spun toward their captive. "You said forty minutes!"

Tim's bloody face split into a slight grin. "It's four minutes. It's code. You're all dead now, sorry."

A black SUV crawled down the access road, its xenon lights cutting through the darkness. Samuel's mind raced what to do? They had to run. "The Jeep. Florence's Jeep. Now!"

They burst through the back door; Collette carrying the taser and Shannon dropping the gun frantically leaving her post of watching Tim. They burst out the back door crouching at the back of the station. They had to get to Florence's jeep. Samuel had seen the car keys in the jeep when he got Buck's gun. The jeep sat twenty yards away, keys dangling from the ignition.

"Down," he hissed at the women as they climbed in. "Stay down."

Samuel slumped behind the wheel as the SUV parked on the side in from of them. Two men appeared – athletic builds, grey sport coats, blue jeans. Professional killers trying to look casual.

The first man drew a pistol, approaching the station. The second circled toward the shed where Buck's body cooled.

Almost like an involuntary reflex Samuel's hand turned on the key and his swollen leg hit the accelerator.

Samuel twisted the key, the engine roaring to life. "Hold on and buckle up!"

"Samuel!" Collette screamed as she secured her seatbelt.

Samuel quickly fastened his seat belt and stomped on the accelerator, the Jeep lurching toward the shed. The second grey suited man turned, firing twice. Glass exploded inward as bullets punched through the windshield.

The jeep caught the grey suited shooter mid-turn, crushing him against the shed wall. Wood on the outside of the shed splintered as his spine snapped.

Gunfire erupted from behind them – the first man had appeared from the station. Bullets shattered the rear window. Shannon and Collette screamed as glass rained down.

Samuel frantically reached for Buck's gun, finding empty air. It was still in the station.

He turned the key again, but the engine only clicked. A bullet must have hit something vital.

Through the spiderwebbed windshield, he saw the second grey suited killer approaching, weapon raised. Time slowed as the man reached the passenger window, gun leveling at Samuel's head.

"Bang!" The shot that came was not from the killer's gun.

The grey suited man's head disappeared in a red mist, his large body crumpling to the ground. Behind him stood Tim, holding Samuel's gun, his hands shaking.

"He... he's dead, it's all over now," Tim stammered.

Samuel kicked the door open, his foot screaming in protest. "Shannon? Collette?"

"We're okay," Collette answered, though blood from flying glass decorated her arms. "We're okay."

In the distance, sirens began to wail, growing louder. Samuel's 911 call had gone through after all.

Tim dropped the gun, raising his hands toward the approaching lights. His shoulders slumped, years of guilt seeming to catch up at once. "I'm sorry," he whispered. "I'm so sorry."

Samuel tried to stand, but his foot gave way. The jeep crash had shattered something – adrenaline had masked the pain until now. He collapsed against the hood, consciousness fading.

The current pulled at him one last time, dark water swirling around his chest. But this time was different. The hand reaching down through the surface was solid and real. Samuel grasped it, feeling warm fingers intertwined with his own.

With surprising strength, the hand pulled him up, breaking him free from the river's grasp. Water cascaded from his clothes as he appeared into brilliant sunlight. And there she was – Monica, radiant in her purple dress, her smile as bright as he remembered from their happiest days.

She did not speak, did not need to. Her eyes said everything: pride, forgiveness, love. She squeezed his hand once more, her touch pure warmth and light. The guilt that had weighed him down like stones in his pockets finally floated away with the current.

Monica's smile widened as she released his hand, stepping back. Not walking away this time – setting him free.

"Samuel?" Collette's voice filtered through the dream. "Samuel, can you hear me?"

His eyes fluttered open to ambulance lights and Collette's concerned face. But he could still feel the warmth of Monica's hand in his, could still see her smile, blessing him to move forward, to live again.

Police cars flooded the clearing, officers appearing with weapons drawn. Tim knelt with his hands behind his head as flashlight beams crisscrossed the scene.

"In there," Samuel managed, pointing toward Station 7. "Florence. Evidence. On the laptop..."

His voice faded as the pain became too much. The river's constant roar had finally gone quiet. It was time to wake up.

***

Red and blue lights painted the canyon walls as law enforcement swarmed Station 7. Samuel watched from the back of the ambulance as officers moved methodically through the scene, their flashlight beams cutting through the pre-dawn darkness.

"Four confirmed deceased," a detective's voice crackled over the radio. "One female inside the station, two males by the shed, one male inside." A pause. "Jesus, someone really went to town with that nail gun."

Through the open ambulance doors, Samuel could see Tim being led away in handcuffs, his shoulders slumped, tears cutting paths through the dirt on his face. Shannon stood with two officers nearby, her hands gesturing as she gave her statement, her nurse's training lending precision to her description of events.

A female detective approached the ambulance, her badge catching the emergency lights. "Mr. Ross? Ms. Bennett?" She glanced at her notepad. "I'm Detective Martinez. We're gathering evidence now, but I wanted you to know – we've had reports of several female hikers going missing from this area over the past few years. Never enough evidence to connect the dots, until now."

Collette's hand tightened around Samuel's. "How many?"

"We're still counting," Martinez said grimly. "The files on that laptop you found... this goes deeper than we imagined." She hesitated. "There's something else. Search and rescue found a body at the bottom of Eagle's Point. Male, late twenties or early thirties."

Samuel closed his eyes. Daniel. Another life lost to Buck's brutality.

"The park service will need statements from both of you," Martinez continued, "but it can wait until you've received medical attention. What you did here tonight – you stopped something terrible. But from what we're seeing in those files, this is just one piece of a much larger operation."

In the ambulance, Samuel fought to stay conscious as paramedics worked on his injuries. Collette sat beside him, her own cuts bandaged, holding his hand.

"The laptop," Samuel said as he navigated through the pain. "Florence kept everything. Years of records, contacts, shipping routes. Heaven's Gifts are not just here – they are everywhere. There must be operation hubs not just here, but all over the country."

Collette squeezed his hand. "You need to heal first, Samuel. This isn't your fight."

"It is now." His voice grew stronger. "All those women, Collette. How many Monicas have they broken? How many lives have they stolen?" He met her eyes. "I was a coward once, calculating odds instead of acting. Never again."

"Then we'll fight together," she said softly. "Shannon and I – we're witnesses now. We can help build the case." Her willpower kicked in, matching his determination.

A flash of purple caught Samuel's attention through the ambulance window – just a flowering bush in the pre-dawn light, but it made him smile. He could almost hear Monica's voice: "Now you're listening to your heart."

The paramedic checked his vitals again as Samuel closed his eyes. The river's roar had been replaced by something else – a sense of purpose, clear and strong as mountain air. Florence's meticulous records would lead them to other trafficking operations, other monsters hiding behind respectable facades. Heaven's Gifts had thought Station 7 was just another transaction point.

Instead, it would be their undoing.

Samuel drifted into sleep, but this time there was no drowning dream. Instead, he saw Monica in her purple dress, standing in sunlight. She smiled at him – not a goodbye smile, but one of blessing. Of release. "Go get them," she whispered, fading into the light.

He would. One case at a time, one rescue at a time, he would tear Heaven's Gifts apart. The lawyer who calculated odds had died in that canyon. In his place was someone new – someone who understood that sometimes justice needed more than just legal briefs and courtroom arguments.

Sometimes it needed a willing heart and bloody hands.

The ambulance turned east, toward sunrise. Toward the next case.

Samuel was ready.

ABOUT THE AUTHOR

Anthony B. Gray is a seasoned attorney with 18 years of experience in both criminal and civil litigation. When not in the courtroom, he balances fatherhood to two young boys with his passion for yoga and fitness. Drawing from his legal background and personal journey, "Torrent" marks his debut novel.

AFTERWORD

While "Torrent" is a work of fiction, suicide and human trafficking are devastating realities affecting countless lives. If you or someone you know needs help, please reach out to these resources.

Suicide Prevention: National Suicide Prevention Lifeline 1-800-273-8255 www.suicidepreventionlifeline.org

Human Trafficking: National Human Trafficking Hotline 1-888-373-7888 www.humantraffickinghotline.org Contact by Text: 233733 (Text "HELP" or "INFO")

If you suspect human trafficking activity, report it to: Department of Homeland Security Tip Line 1-866-347-2423 www.ice.gov/tips